THE GREATEST SHOW IN THE GALAXY

DOCTOR WHO
THE GREATEST SHOW IN THE GALAXY

based on the BBC television series by Stephen Wyatt
by arrangement with BBC Books, a division of BBC
Enterprises Ltd

STEPHEN WYATT

Number 144 in the
Target Doctor Who Library

published by
the Paperback Division of
W H Allen & Co Plc

A Target Book
Published in 1989
By the Paperback Division of
W H Allen & Co Plc
Sekforde House, 175/9 St John Street, London EC1V 4LL

The BBC producer was John Nathan-Turner
The director was Alan Wareing
The role of the Doctor was played by Sylvester McCoy

Printed and bound in Great Britain by
Cox & Wyman Ltd, Reading

ISBN 0 426 20341 0

CONTENTS

Overture

It had an atmosphere all of its own. You sensed that the moment you entered. It was not a particularly big circus, nor a particularly smart one. The sawdust ring was emblazoned with the words:

THE GREATEST SHOW IN THE GALAXY

but the brightly coloured lettering was starting to fade and there was not enough room in the ring for a really spectacular act. An elephant, for example, could never have fitted. Only human beings or would-be human beings could perform there with any ease.

The seating, too, was on the cramped side, wooden benches rising steeply up the side of the tent from the ringside. You could never have got a large audience in there, however tightly you crammed the people in – not that there ever seemed to be huge crowds fighting their way in.

There was a place for a small band but no band was ever seen playing there. Instead, over the slightly crackling loudspeaker system came bright cheerful music of the sort you'd expect to find in a circus – in an ordinary circus, that is.

The clowns, however, were undoubtedly impressive when they entered to a tinny fanfare to start the show. Cartwheeling and somersaulting and stilt-walking and juggling with an almost unreal precision, their white clown faces smiled and smiled all the time, as though the spectacular stunts they were performing cost them absolutely no effort.

The Ringmaster was impressive too in his way when he finally made his entrance into the ring. He was a tall, imposing man, dressed in a glittering blue and red coat and striped trousers, and wearing on his head an elegant red top hat. In his hand he held a long snake-like whip, the traditional symbol of a ringmaster's authority, but wielded by this Ringmaster with particular speed and dexterity.

The Ringmaster always acknowledged his audience with confidence as well, standing there isolated in the ring by a powerful white follow-spot. You felt that the whole proceedings would be effortlessly controlled by the sharp crack of his flickering whip. There was perhaps something slightly disturbing about his smile, something forced, even sardonic about it, and about the look in his eyes too. But you might well decide you were being oversensitive, affected by the strangeness of the atmosphere, by that unusual feeling you couldn't quite put your finger on.

And then the Ringmaster would begin to speak. He spoke in a soft but penetrating voice, the rhythm of his words backed by a barely perceptible musical beat issuing from the speakers. The Ringmaster was a cool customer, no doubt about that; not the blustering braggart of the traditional circus, but someone who knew the way the galaxy operates and accepts it with a shrug. He was doing a job and he was doing it very well but somehow he was letting you know it was just a job, perhaps a job he'd been doing too long. Or so it might seem to you if you were starting to let the atmosphere of the circus get through to you again.

The words he spoke, however, were friendly enough and when you heard them, you would probably feel your doubts put to rest.

'Now welcome, folks, and I'm sure you'd like to know,
We're at the start of one big circus show.
There are acts that are cool and acts that will amaze,
Acts that are plain scary and acts that will simply daze.
Acts of all sorts that will make you all agree

It's the Greatest Show in the Galaxy . . .'

The words continued smoothly, winningly, as the Ringmaster's confident but oddly inexpressive eyes ranged over the seating banks seeking to meet those of his audience.

'There's lots of surprises for all the family
In the Greatest Show in the Galaxy.
So many strange surprises I'm prepared to bet . . .'

And then, just as you were settling back comfortably in your seat – or as comfortably as the benches allowed – and looking forward to enjoying the show, there would be a pause. The Ringmaster would hold the pause and then, staring his unseen audience full in the face, he would complete his final couplet, hissing out the last words.

'Whatever you've seen before,' he'd announce to the strangely silent circus, 'you ain't seen nothing yet.'

And at that moment, in the unlikely event that any of you ever were visitors to the Greatest Show in the Galaxy, you would probably start to wish you had decided to stay at home and watch television instead.

1

Beginners

Deep space. No planets, just stars.

A small speck appears among the stars. A faint distorted bleeping noise. The speck comes nearer. The bleeping increases in volume.

It is a metallic double-sphered artificial satellite with a large round body and smaller round head. Suddenly on the head of the satellite, two small lights flash on like two tiny, sinister red eyes. They have detected the presence of some other object hurtling by through deep space.

That object is the TARDIS. The satellite has sensed its approach and now its little red eyes wink out again.

The Doctor had been in an odd mood for some time. Ace had got used to the fact that the Doctor was always being seized by sudden whims or weird ideas that she could not understand but it still annoyed her. Particularly when the mood in question seemed to involve practising conjuring tricks and juggling with coloured balls, and even more particularly when Ace was turning the TARDIS inside out trying to find something. It wasn't in her rucksack. It wasn't in the control room. It wasn't anywhere at all that she could see in the whole TARDIS. Eventually there was only one course left open to her: to beard the apparently totally engrossed Doctor for an explanation.

She found him in the control room, juggling small balls of all colours, a look of rapt concentration on his face.

Ace took a deep breath. 'Doctor,' she began, 'where's my nitro-nine?'

'Isn't it in your rucksack?' the Doctor replied, looking as if cosmic butter wouldn't melt in his mouth. He added yet another ball, a red one, to the three or four already passing nimbly from hand to hand.

'It was.' Ace returned suspiciously. She'd mixed some more nitro-nine after their last adventure in case of emergencies. She knew she had. She also knew that the Doctor did not really approve of her tendency to tackle all their problems by lobbing powerful explosives at them.

'Things don't just vanish,' she grumbled.

'No,' the Doctor agreed. Though, as he spoke, unless Ace was very much deceived, he threw the new red ball up in the air and it vanished – literally vanished into thin air. It was probably an optical illusion; or a conjuring trick. It certainly didn't seem to surprise the Doctor. Nor did it help Ace to get to the bottom of what had happened to her nitro-nine.

'You've bunged it down the waste disposal, haven't you, Professor?' she accused. Without thinking she had slipped into calling the Doctor by the title she knew annoyed him though she herself preferred it. But even this slip did not appear to ruffle the Doctor's serenity. He juggled on.

'Now, Ace, would I do a sly, underhand thing like that?' he replied sweetly.

'You would if you thought it'd keep me out of trouble,' Ace retorted hotly.

Perhaps it was the word 'trouble' that did it. Perhaps it was just one of those very odd coincidences that seemed to plague life with the Doctor. Whatever the reason, a warning signal on the TARDIS' observation screen erupted at this very moment, filling the control room with its shrill bleeping.

'Trouble,' the Doctor exclaimed smugly, almost as if he had been expecting it and merely filling in time with the juggling. He let the coloured balls – or at least those that were left of them – tumble to the floor, and went over to the observation screen. Ace joined him there.

11

On the screen they could see a small metallic double-sphered satellite of unusual construction. They could also make out two tiny red lights, flickering on and off.

'What is it, Professor?' Ace demanded.

The Doctor shrugged. 'Some fairly rudimentary artificial satellite, I imagine. Nothing very remarkable.' He paused, his forehead wrinkling with thought. 'Except, of course, that it's so near the TARDIS.'

Even as he spoke, the satellite grew still nearer and its two lights became like little eyes searching them out.

'Is it supposed to get that close, Professor?' Ace watched its progress with concern.

'No,' the Doctor reassured her. 'But it won't penetrate the TARDIS' defence system.' A sudden doubt struck him. 'Unless, of course, Ace . . .'

'I haven't touched the defence system,' Ace returned hotly. It was just like the Professor to try to blame her. Sometimes she thought that he'd prefer to travel with somebody without an inquiring mind, someone who'd never try to find out how anything worked. She felt doubly aggrieved this time, since she'd been wanting to take the TARDIS' defence system apart for some time now and hadn't yet been able to get round to it.

'Well, if you haven't,' the Doctor retorted, 'then any second now, the satellite should . . .'

But the satellite did not do as it was supposed to do. It did not blow up. It was not deflected from its chosen course. It carried on implacably getting nearer and nearer to the TARDIS. The Doctor seemed alarmed for the first time.

'I don't understand,' he murmured. 'It's penetrated the first line of the defence system.'

'There's a second one then?' Ace enquired.

'Of course,' the Doctor replied proudly. 'And that will undoubtedly . . .'

But the satellite still did not do as it was supposed to do. It did not explode. It was not diverted from its course. It just came nearer and nearer to the TARDIS, until it was so close that its metallic body filled the whole of the observation screen and the bleeping from the alarm signal became almost deafening. The Doctor and Ace both put their hands over their ears to protect them from the din.

'Maybe I should have had a go at the defence systems, Professor.'

'Pardon?' Ace was shouting as loud as she could but the Doctor didn't appear to hear her. Maybe he doesn't want to hear me, Ace thought, and then dismissed the notion as unworthy.

She decided to try again, shouting with all her might. 'I said, maybe I should have . . .'

Suddenly, mysteriously, there was silence. The observation screen was blank. The satellite had disappeared. Outside the stars were eternally twinkling in space and that, apparently, was all.

'Danger over,' the Doctor announced, breathing a sigh of relief.

Then suddenly they heard a noise. A peculiar noise; a very peculiar noise. They turned and there in a far corner of the TARDIS was the metallic satellite, its little red eyes winking on and off. It was not, in fact, all that big, but it was a shock to see it nevertheless.

'How extraordinary!' the Doctor exclaimed. 'It's materialized *inside* the TARDIS.'

'Is that unusual?' Ace enquired.

'Almost without precedent,' the Doctor replied solemnly. And before Ace could rush towards the satellite to examine it, he placed a restraining hand on her shoulder. There were tests to be done, checks to be made, before he would allow Ace or anyone else near the alien object.

The instruments were to hand easily enough, emerging mostly from the Doctor's apparently endlessly capacious pockets, and the tests took only a few minutes, but to someone as young and impatient as Ace those minutes seemed more like hours.

'After all,' the Doctor warned, 'it might be some kind of bomb.'

Ace perked up immediately. 'If it is, can I keep it?'

'Certainly not,' the Doctor retorted. The inspection over, he replaced the measuring implements inside his coat pocket. 'Well, it seems pretty harmless to me,' he pronounced, to Ace's disappointment. 'Just what you'd expect in this part of the Galaxy.'

The confident words were scarcely out of the Doctor's mouth when the satellite apparently decided to prove him wrong. It sprouted eight metallic legs and scuttled, spider-like, towards the console of the TARDIS. And, while Ace and the Doctor were still recovering from their surprise, the satellite shot a snake-like wire from its head and plugged itself into the console.

Eventually Ace spoke. 'Was that just as you'd expect too, Professor?'

'Not entirely,' the Doctor returned drily. Whatever the satellite was programmed to do and whoever had programmed it, the full attention of Ace and the Doctor was now assured. They did not have to wait long for enlightenment.

The TARDIS viewing screen suddenly erupted into life. On it was a picture of a striped circus tent set in the middle of a beautiful, lush, green meadow. That picture was followed by others, equally glowing, depicting various circus acts – clowns, jugglers, acrobats, accompanied with an irritatingly ingratiating voice, the sort of smoothy voice Ace associated with hundreds of television commercials back on Earth.

'Yes, it's Festival Time at the Psychic Circus – the Greatest Show in the Galaxy!' the voice announced to a tinny fanfare. 'So why not come along and have the time of your life?'

After all the excitement and mystery, the let-down was too much for Ace. 'I just don't believe it,' she grumbled. 'Junk mail. We used to get mounds of the stuff through the

14

letter-box. And now you're being bombarded with it inside the TARDIS.'

'Junk mail gets everywhere,' the Doctor agreed philosophically. Ace could have gone on grumbling in the same vein for some time but the Doctor gestured her to be silent.

'There are big prizes, too, for the best new circus acts,' the voice was proclaiming in its smarmy way. 'No wonder travellers from all over the galaxy make their way to the planet Segonax for the Festival. Remember, whether you want to watch or compete, there's a great time for you on the planet Segonax. The planet has an Earthlike telluric atmosphere and, what is more, easy access via our special polyportable landing base . . .'

To illustrate these last words, an image appeared of a gleaming silver disc-shaped structure, again set in a verdant landscape of trees, bushes and flowers. Obviously this was the landing base in question.

'Now as for the Circus itself . . .'

Ace had had enough. The disappointment had been bad enough, but now it seemed as if the junk mail satellite was never going to stop going on about the delights of this Psychic Circus or whatever it was. She walked smartly over to the console and pulled the satellite's wires from it. The smarmy voice stopped in mid-sentence with satisfying finality.

The Doctor stared at the blank screen. 'I thought you'd have been interested in going to the circus, Ace.'

'Nah.' Ace shook her head contemptuously. 'Kids' stuff. I went once. They didn't even have any tigers. It was naff and it was boring.' She paused. 'Apart from the clowns, of course.'

'Oh?' The Doctor was alert. 'You found them funny?'

Ace shook her head even more vigorously. 'No, creepy.' As she spoke, she shuddered a little. It had been one of the very few times in her childhood when something had really scared her. Perhaps it was the fact that you never saw the clown's real face. Or was it the fact that clowns smiled, whatever happened and whatever they did, because their smiles were forever painted on? No; no clowns, thank you very much, Ace thought to herself. She hoped the Doctor hadn't noticed her little shudder. It was bad for her image.

Apparently he hadn't. He was more interested in defending circuses in general. 'I do think you're being unfair, Ace. Many of the acts require a great deal of skill and courage. You should appreciate that.' A faraway look came into his eyes, a look he often had when his thoughts were one step ahead of Ace's and he wasn't letting her in on them. 'As a matter of fact, I quite fancy the Festival talent contest myself.'

'Leave it out.' Ace was anxious to change the subject now to anything but clowns and circuses. But it was not to be. The satellite decided to make a contribution to the discussion by once more plugging itself into the console. Its challenging voice rang out before Ace could stop it..

'Scared?' The smarminess was gone now.

'What?' Ace turned to face her accuser angrily.

'I said, are you scared to come to the Psychic Circus?' the voice repeated in a still more mocking tone.

'No,' Ace retorted hotly. 'Course not.'

'Scared to take part then?'

'No,' Ace countered. There was nothing more likely to get her back up than a suggestion that she was a coward.

'Well, if you are,' the voice jeered, 'then go ahead, ignore me. I quite understand.' And without another word, it unplugged itself and the little red eyes went out for the last time.

Ace was aware of the Doctor's piercing eyes studying her. Perhaps he had noticed that little shudder. At any rate, the scrutiny made her uncomfortable. 'I don't believe it,' she remarked to cover her embarrassment, 'Junk mail that talks back.'

'Shall we throw it away then and forget about it?' the Doctor enquired with just a hint of smugness. 'After all, I'm sure the Psychic Circus isn't scary at all. They all came

16

from Earth originally anyway. It's just a teaser to get us to go.'

The Doctor was handing her an excuse to forget the whole thing. Yet in a way, knowing her stubborn self-sufficiency, the Doctor was also making it very difficult for her to back out. After all, it was just a circus.

She decided to take it out on the satellite. 'OK, you win, junkbox,' she told it wearily. 'I'm not scared of anything.'

Which, as she was to discover, was not entirely true.

2

Welcome to Segonax

They had been running for hours and Bellboy was exhausted. He felt he could not run any further and he was beginning to lose hope. When he caught his foot on a piece of scrub and fell headlong on to a dusty dirt-track, he had almost given up. He lay there unmoving, helpless, his still young, open face lined with fatigue and grimed with dust and sweat, his bright hippy clothes, the braided yellow military jacket, the purple bell-bottomed trousers, faded by the sun and ripped by the bushes.

Without Flowerchild he would probably never have moved from the spot. She had always been the stronger of the two, right from the beginning, and now she knelt by him and tried to urge him from his despair. Her multi-coloured, flower-patterned dress was in no better shape than Bellboy's clothes; her face was young and attractive, and although it showed signs of suffering and tiredness, her determination still shone through.

'Come on, Bellboy,' she urged, quietly but firmly. 'We can't give up now.'

Bellboy shook his head wearily, his eyes turning listlessly back the way they had come. 'They'll catch us, Flowerchild, I know it. They'll catch us and drag us back to the Circus.'

Flowerchild placed one hand firmly on his shoulder. 'Bellboy, please. You promised. You know it's down to us now. We're the only ones left to fight.'

Bellboy knew it was true. If they did not succeed in what they had planned to do then the future was indeed bleak. They had been planning their escape for weeks. It had not

18

been easy to find an opportunity to slip away and it had been even harder for Bellboy to convince himself that their desperate plan could work. In those first moments of freedom, when every step took them away from the Circus, he had believed it was possible. But not now. Not after the endless futile running up and down the sun-baked hills without getting any nearer their goal.

Then, as if to confirm his despair, he looked up into the sky and saw what he most feared. Two brightly coloured kites fluttered up above them. But there was nothing casual about their fluttering. They were there for a purpose, seeking something out. Painted on both sides, the kites carried a large eye symbol. It was a symbol Bellboy knew all too well, had come to hate for all that it represented. What little energy Flowerchild had given him evaporated at the sight. 'Your kites, Flowerchild,' he murmured brokenly, 'your beautiful kites.'

'We mustn't think of that now,' Flowerchild insisted. 'Come on!'

Somehow, miraculously, she willed him to his feet again and they started to run. They ran in the hope that the kites would not be able to follow them, and that those who used the kites to seek them out would eventually abandon the search. It was a small hope, of course, but it was their only hope.

The sleek black hearse pulled noiselessly to a stop. The elegant limousine was an incongruous sight amid the barren dust-tracks and parched shrubland, but nothing like as incongruous as its occupants. Their clothes were appropriate enough: the black frock-coats and suits and black-ribboned top hats associated with undertakers everywhere. The clothes would have been quite enough to convince a passer-by that these were men going about their proper business in the appropriate vehicle. That was, in part, their purpose.

But when a couple of them got out, the full incongruity

became apparent. For these undertakers had clowns' faces and the leader, a tall, commanding figure, had a bright red gash of a smile painted across his face at odds not just with his costume but also with the cold blue of the eyes that stood out in the white mask of his make-up. It was a face in which genuine emotion was impossible to read. It was a face both cruel and impassive.

The leader studied the sky for a moment. Kites fluttered there, but they were not telling him what he wanted to know. He turned to his companion, a shorter, deferential figure, who pressed the button on a tracking device. A shrill intermittent bleeping was transmitted through it from the kites. They had lost track of what the leader wanted so much to find. He made a sudden gesture of impatience. But as suddenly his mood changed. The bleeping sound had become deeper and more sustained. Some of the kites, at least, had homed in on their prey.

Satisfied, the leader gave a cruel smile and gestured to his companion to switch off the tracking device and get back into the large black limousine.

Soon the hearse was speeding along the dirt-track in pursuit of the kites. And, of course, in pursuit of what the kites themselves were pursuing.

It was a game of cat and mouse, and Bellboy had no illusions about who were the mice. Each time they thought they had left the kites behind, after some complex piece of doubling back on their tracks, bought at the expense of one more scrap of their failing energy, there they would be in the sky again, fluttering away, the eye symbol plainly visible, so beautiful and yet so dangerous. His despair was never very far away now, even though he had been running as fast as he could to be with his beloved Flowerchild.

Even Flowerchild was beginning to doubt their chances of ever totally evading the kites. But, unlike Bellboy, she had found a solution. It was a painful solution and that was why they stood for the moment irresolute and sad by

20

the roadside. Flowerchild had explained to Bellboy, sadly and reluctantly, that they would have to split up. 'There's no choice,' she urged, the desolation of the landscape now matching the desolation of their mood. They had loved each other for so many years and now they faced the prospect of parting perhaps for ever.

But even Bellboy saw the force of her argument. The kites would keep on tracking them, but if one of them drew the kites after them then the other, unobserved, might perhaps get where they needed to go.

'One of us must get there,' Flowerchild insisted, holding Bellboy's hand tenderly.

'And the other one?'

There was no way of answering that, and fortunately no need to answer, since they both knew the risks. In any case, Flowerchild was too full of pent-up feeling to be able to speak. Instead she kissed Bellboy impulsively on the cheek and reached with her free hand to her ear. From it she removed one of her earrings. It had a sharp-edged angular design. She had made it for herself years ago during the good times. In their talks they often remembered the day she had made this particular pair of earrings because it had been the last truly happy day of their lives.

'I want you to have this,' Flowerchild insisted, pressing it into Bellboy's hand. He took it without protest. If he was not to be with Flowerchild then at least he would always have a memento of her. Perhaps one day he would even return it to her ear and make the pair complete again.

'I'll wait here a while.' Bellboy spoke fluently now, anxious to hide how much he dreaded losing her. 'Then I'll take the long route. That should draw them after me.' He had assumed the role of decoy without discussion and Flowerchild knew it made sense. She had the energy and will to make it to their destination; he did not.

'No silly risks now,' she urged with a sad smile. Bellboy nodded. They both knew there could be no time for long farewells. He urged her away before the kites found them again.

One quick kiss and Flowerchild reluctantly turned away and started to walk away up the track. One wave and she started to run. One final look back and she was gone.

Bellboy looked up into the sky. She had got away before the kites had rediscovered them. 'Come on, kites,' he whispered to the empty sky above. 'Find me. It's me you want.'

And a black hearse continued to speed smoothly through the bleak landscape in pursuit of its double prey.

The planet Segonax did not live up to its publicity, but then few things did, Ace thought. The terrain was bleak and arid, the sun unrelentingly hot and there wasn't a tree or blade of grass in sight. The Doctor, as usual, was too eager to explore the new territory to do anything except look on the bright side.

'I've heard good reports of the friendliness of the natives,' he assured Ace, as they stood surveying the landscape.

'So where's this landing base they talked about?' Ace protested.

'Oh, I expect that's for those not fortunate enough to possess a TARDIS,' the Doctor beamed.

'So now where, Professor?'

'Over there, I think,' the Doctor pointed ahead of him, up a dusty lane, to a distant figure. 'We'll ask for directions.'

Ace shrugged. The Doctor had decided they should come here and so the Doctor could decide how to handle it. Therefore she dutifully followed the Doctor up the lane.

The figure that sat there was no more welcoming than the landscape, or so Ace thought. She was a large, truculent-looking woman, dressed in brightly coloured but shabby clothes, her hat decorated with rather incongruous feathers. She was some sort of stallholder. That much was clear from the produce laid out on the roadside before her, and the horse and cart behind her. But when Ace took a look at the produce, she was not entirely surpised that there seemed to be a shortage of customers. It consisted entirely of large, bulbous vegetables and fruit of a size and shape Ace had never seen before, all of them with skins of the most lurid shades of blue, yellow and purple.

The woman watched their approach impassively, perhaps even aggressively. But the Doctor was not to be deterred when he wanted to find something out. He politely raised his hat and gave an especially charming smile before wishing the stallholder good afternoon and introducing himself and Ace.

There was a long pause while the woman studied them both dubiously, before she eventually deigned to speak. 'What sort of costume do you call that?' she finally demanded from the Doctor, staring balefully at him.

'I don't understand.'

She turned her gaze to Ace. 'And hers is no better.' She pursed her lips disapprovingly. 'We don't want your type round here.'

The Doctor was undeterred. 'And what type might that be?'

'Weirdos,' the woman snapped. 'You can tell them at a glance, you know.'

'I didn't actually,' replied the Doctor mildly. Ace tried to catch his eye. This would teach him to promise circus fun and friendly natives. She was beginning to enjoy trying to guess how the Doctor was going to get round this immovable object. For his part, the Doctor had obviously decided on a tactical retreat. But, before doing so, he bought some of the disgusting fruit. Two of the largest and most bulbous specimens on the whole stall, one for him and one for Ace.

He withdrew a short distance from the stall carrying his purchases and then, to Ace's disgust, handed her one of the fruit and told her to get eating.

'You mean, we're actually going to eat this muck?' Ace demanded.

'It's elementary diplomacy,' the Doctor explained in an undertone. 'She apparently thinks we are a pair of undesirable intergalactic hippies. We have to convince her that we are nice, clean-living people who eat lots of fresh fruit and pay our way.'

'Paying good money for this muck is daylight robbery,' Ace protested as she took her first bite. The fruit tasted every bit as unpleasant as it looked. 'Do you expect me to finish this?'

'Every last bite,' the Doctor assured her, with just a hint of malicious pleasure in his voice. 'After all, we want the charming lady to tell us how to find this Circus, don't we?' And he turned and gave the woman a cheery wave. 'Delicious, madam, quite delicious,' he shouted to her. The stallholder showed no sign of having heard him but he kept smiling winningly none the less.

'Bet she gets something decent for tea when she gets home,' Ace grumbled. 'I bet even her horse gets something better than this.' But, despite her grumbling, Ace did manage to force the fruit down, mouthful by unappetizing mouthful. However, by the end she was feeling fairly ill, unlike the Doctor who seemed actually to enjoy his fruit. Indeed, the moment he had finished it, he bounced back to the stall with his face still wreathed in smiles.

'More?'

Even the Doctor blanched for a moment. 'Er, no, thank you,' he managed to reply politely. 'It was delicious but extremely filling.' He cleared his throat. 'By now I am sure you will have gathered, dear lady, that we are not the sort of hobbledehoys and vagabonds you take such exception to. Indeed, as I said when I introduced myself, I am known as the Doctor.'

The stallholder sniffed. 'Some people'll call themselves anything.'

The Doctor thought it best to ignore this remark. 'Be

24

that as it may, madam, we would appreciate your help. We are looking for . . .'

But he never got to finish the sentence. His voice was drowned out by the sound of an approaching motorcycle. He and Ace both turned in the direction of the rapidly nearing traveller.

Nord, the Vandal of the Roads, was in a good mood. He was on his way to the gig at the Psychic Circus. His bike was going like a dream. Using the landing base had been even easier than he could have imagined. And he had just consumed two of his favourite enormous multi-layer, ket-chup-smeared, meat-filled sandwiches for lunch.

He was a big man was Nord, and he put away a great deal of food. If he whizzed by you in a country lane on his bike with its fearsome animal horns on the front, you would have got a blurred impression of big muscles, large tattoos, masses of black leather clothing, a brutal unshaven face and a fearsome Viking-style crash-helmet on his head. That fleeting glance was probably the best way to see Nord. He was not a man with many hidden depths to his character, and what was apparent on the surface was really quite threatening. People normally did not get into arguments with Nord the Vandal, and those that did lived to regret it.

Nord's good moods never lasted, so it was a pity nobody had encountered him while he was in one. This particular good mood was destined to come to a very abrupt end. Just as he was hurtling down the lane past the stall, his bike started to give out strange spluttering sounds. Then, almost without warning, the engine shuddered to a complete halt and he was left ignominiously stranded on a stationary motorbike.

Nord was furious. The bike was his pride and joy. How dare it break down on him! He heaved his considerable bulk off the saddle and pulled out his toolbox angrily and noisily. The tools spilled on to the road. He picked up a gigantic spanner and started to investigate the problem.

His repair methods depended more on brute strength than any particular mechanical skill.

'Need a hand?' Nord looked up threateningly to see a girl standing by him. 'I reckon it could be a stuck valve,' she continued.

'Get lost!' Nord did not want anybody interfering with his bike, let alone some stupid girl who didn't know what she was talking about.

'It's a great bike.' Ace continued admiringly.

'Clear off.' Nord stood up and his huge frame loomed ominously over her. 'Clear off. Or I'll get nasty. Very nasty.'

Ace shrugged, unintimidated. 'Well, if you don't want to save yourself some time it's up to you.' She took a closer look. 'Course, it could be a valve spring.'

'Scram! Or I'll do something horrible to your ears.' Nord screamed so loudly and so fiercely that even Ace decided it would be better not to pursue the conversation.

'Suit yourself,' she said, striding coolly back towards the Doctor and the stall. 'And I hope your big end goes,' she murmured secretly to herself as she went, leaving Nord struggling furiously with the largest set of spanners had ever seen.

The Doctor, meanwhile, was still trying to pump the stallholder for information. 'He'll be going there,' she announced, nodding at Nord. 'They all go there.'

'Go where?' enquired the Doctor.

'The Psychic Circus, of course,' answered the woman as if she could not believe anyone could ask such a stupid question. 'All the riff-raff go there. Infernal Extraterrestrials like him. Monopods from Lelex.' She paused before delivering her final insult. 'Doctors.'

The Doctor frowned. 'I don't understand. You're saying he's going to the Circus?'

The stallholder nodded. 'Course. Anybody who's up to no good goes there. We locals wouldn't touch it with a bargepole.'

26

'Is it far, this, er, appalling spectacle?' the Doctor pursued, trying to keep the right tone of disapproval in his voice.

'Miles and miles,' the stallholder replied smugly. 'Why do you think that lout over there has got that noisy monstrosity polluting the countryside.' She eyed the Doctor suspiciously. 'Here, *you* aren't thinking of going there, are you?'

'No, no, the very idea,' the Doctor returned hastily. 'But if you could just excuse me for a moment.' He hastened towards where Ace stood, from a distance observing Nord making a real hash of repairing his bike.

'Any chance of a lift, do you think, Ace?'

'Worth a try, I suppose. He doesn't look after that bike, you know. If he'd let me . . .'

'Yes, yes, Ace, never mind,' the Doctor interjected, cutting off a potential lecture on motorbike maintenance before it got under way. 'Let's just concentrate on getting to the Circus, shall we?'

They walked towards Nord under the still suspicious eyes of the stallholder. Much to Ace's surprise, Nord seemed to have finished his repairs and was packing away his tools prior to departure.

The Doctor was all charm. 'Excuse me, if you're going to the Circus, I wondered if you might give us a lift and . . .'

Nord drew himself up to his full height and bulk and stood there, towering over the Doctor.

'Do you want something really horrible doing to your nose?'

'Not really,' the Doctor answered mildly. 'It's just that . . .'

'Nobody gets lifts from Nord, the Vandal of the Roads. Nobody! Understand?'

The Doctor looked up into the brutal face that glared down on him. 'If you say so.'

'Now listen, pugface . . .' Ace was all for intervening and explaining to Nord what a very important person the

27

Doctor was and how he should be honoured to carry him, but it was perhaps a good thing for her physical well-being that Nord did not wait to hear her protests. He pulled himself back on to his bike, started it up and roared away with the maximum of noise and smoke.

The Doctor watched him go. 'We don't seem to be getting very far. Literally.'

But Ace was listening for something. 'I bet he still hasn't fixed that valve properly,' she murmured. At that very moment, she heard a violent backfiring from the receding bike. She had been right. It was the first thing that had happened to her on Segonax to give her any pleasure at all.

'Come on, over here!'

The kites never left him now. And Bellboy kept on shouting to them to make quite sure they never would again.

'It's me, Bellboy! That's who you're looking for, isn't it?'

He walked on through the parched shrub. He knew that a sleek black limousine would be getting ever closer to him and he knew who would be in it. But that didn't matter, as long as Flowerchild was all right.

Flowerchild came over the brow of the hill and looked down into the dusty valley below. The bus was just where they had abandoned it all those years ago. It was weather-beaten now but she could still make out its garish psyche-delic colours and the places where each of them had signed their name and scrawled a simple self-portrait in bright, splodgy paint. Her picture would be there. And Bellboy's. And all the others'. But it was best not to think of them.

She clambered down the steep slope and into the valley. As she came closer to the bus, she could see the welcoming slogan from their travelling days:
THE ROAD IS OPEN AND THE RIDES ARE FREE.
Not that the bus would ever move again now. It was embedded in the sand and its back wheels were gone for

28

good. Nevertheless, Flowerchild felt a rush of affection for the old jalopy as she finally reached its side. She even spent a few precious moments gazing at the portraits of herself and Bellboy, together even then.

But there was urgent work to be done. She clambered up the crumbling steps, pulled open the door of the driver's cabin and climbed in. It took her a while to find what she wanted among the pedals and controls. Then, suddenly, she remembered what she had to do, pulled one of the controls, and there it was.

She left the cabin, carefully carrying a small metal chest. It was decorated with the symbols from the good old times that Bellboy had painted on it. Finding a clear space, Flowerchild knelt and started to try to wrench the chest open.

Perhaps it was best that she was so preoccupied with opening the chest. Perhaps it was best that she never knew what was coming up behind her until it was too late.

'Hold tight, please.'

A metal hand reached forward and grabbed her throat from behind. She did not have time to struggle or protest.

It was all over.

3

Captain Cook

The sun beat inexorably down on them as they made their way along one of the dusty lanes that seemed to form the only roads on the Planet Segonax. It was heavy going.

'There's something not quite right about all this,' the Doctor mused.

'You're telling me.' Ace retorted. 'Arriving in a machine that can travel through all of time and space, and then having to foot it across miles of countryside to get where we want to go.'

'I was thinking of the atmosphere,' the Doctor returned mildly. 'Segonax was supposed to have been a green and pleasant land once. It used to be known for its remarkably tolerant and easy-going ways.'

'Now they bite your head off as soon as look at you.'

'Precisely.'

'Well,' Ace said, pausing to wipe the sweat from her brow, 'I wouldn't be too chuffed if I kept getting visitors like Nord the Vandal, I suppose.'

'That's true,' the Doctor agreed. 'But then you'd hardly expect a hard case like him to be going to a circus anyway.'

'Perhaps he was conned by that advertising teaser,' Ace remarked. 'Like I was.'

The Doctor refused to rise to the bait. 'Something evil has happened here. I can feel it,' he insisted.

'To do with the Circus?' Ace queried.

If the Doctor knew the answer to her question, he did not get a chance to give it. For ahead of them was an extraordinary landscape of startlingly blue pools of water dotted across an expanse of almost white sand. And, as Ace pointed out, in the midst of all this, two small figures could be made out.

Curiosity moved them both nearer. As they approached, they could start to make out that the two figures were a man and a girl. The man, dressed in khaki explorer's costume and with a topi on his head, was red faced, middle-aged and had a bristling white moustache. The girl was rather harder to place. Even on first impressions she had an almost animal quality but her gear, Ace recognized, was not far from that of a well-dressed punk.

Fragments of their conversation floated through the air. Or rather, of the man's monologue, since the girl seemed to be silently hard at work digging at something in the sand. Behind them a jeep and a gleaming new tent showed that these people were well equipped for whatever it was they were doing.

What they were doing seemed to be some sort of excavation. Or rather, the girl did the excavating while the man delivered a lecture on the subject, or so it seemed to Ace. Still, at least they looked reasonably friendly.

'Of course, on certain planets,' the man's booming voice proclaimed, 'Treops, for example, sights like this are common. You learn to take them for granted. I can remember, on one of my trips to Neogorgon, I came across a whole valley full of electronic dogs' heads submerged in mud. Some sort of primitive burglar alarm system, I suppose, fallen into disuse. I was probably the first person to have visited that valley for several millennia at the very least. So something like this, which to the ordinary dull old stop-at-home might seem quite extraordinary, is just run-of-the-mill as far as I'm concerned. Still, since you've never . . .'

His voice trailed away. The girl, more sensitive to her surroundings, had suddenly tensed. She had at last detected the approach of the Doctor and Ace. Her first reaction was to grasp the shovel she had been using, brandishing it like

31

a weapon. But she lowered it when the Doctor advanced with a smile on his face and his hat raised. The initial impression that these were the friendliest people they had yet met on Segonax was, to Ace's relief, confirmed.

'Greetings. I am the Doctor. And this is Ace.'

'Mags.' The girl spoke quietly, almost reluctantly, as if speech was not her natural form of expression. The same could not be said of the man, who advanced to meet the Doctor, his hand outstretched and a rather self-satisfied smile on his face.

'And I,' he announced with great pride, 'am Captain Cook, the eminent intergalactic explorer. You have no doubt heard of me.'

Ace and the Doctor had not, but were thankful to be spared the embarrassment of admitting it. For from the excavation site itself came a plaintive mechanical voice.

'Let me out please . . . let me out please . . .'

The voice belonged to a large robot head lying half uncovered in the sand. Whether there was a robot body as well was impossible to tell. But the head was huge and its crude metallic features were somehow at odds with the sweet, plaintive voice that continuously begged to be set free.

The Captain, however, seemed only too happy to suspend work for a while and offer them a cup of tea. It was Mags who actually got things ready, but still the thought was there, Ace supposed. And any sort of liquid refreshment on such a hot day was welcome.

As tea was being prepared, it became increasingly clear that Captain Cook not only liked things his own way but also liked everyone to know how much he had seen and how many places he had visited. Ace found it all rather boring but the Doctor seemed happy to sit and play along with his reminiscences, though he could not resist a dig now and then at the Captain's amiable pomposities.

'My own special blend, of course,' the Captain confided when the tea was finally served and he and the Doctor were seated under the tent awning drinking it. 'I take it every-where.' He sipped some more. 'I bet you'll never guess the blend, Doctor.'

The Doctor sipped his tea thoughtfully. 'Well,' he concluded, 'I could be wrong, of course, but isn't it from the Groz Valley on Melagophon?'

'Good, very good, Doctor,' the Captain returned, trying very hard to hide the fact that he was extremely peeved that the Doctor had guessed correctly. He took his irritation out on Mags instead, ordering her back to work on the excavation of the head. Ace, who hated sitting still anyway, eagerly offered to help her. The Doctor's instincts were to restrain Ace from participation until they knew more. But she ran off too quickly and the Doctor was left to enjoy the conversation of Captain Cook.

'Were you ever on Melagophon, Doctor?' he enquired, then continued, without waiting for the Doctor's answer. 'The Frozen Pits of Overod are worth seeing, of course, though much overrated I feel. All right for the trainee explorer but old hands like myself need something a bit more exotic.

'Why come here then?' The Doctor's sharp question cut right across the Captain's train of thought and it took him a moment to think of his answer. Whether it was a true answer or not, of course, the Doctor had no way of telling.

'Well,' Captain Cook began, 'I'm told the Psychic Circus is quite an interesting little show, particularly at this time when everybody turns up to compete in the Festival. Besides, Mags wanted to come.'

'You always travel together?'

'Of late, yes,' the Captain agreed. 'I found her on the planet Vulpana.' He leaned confidentially across to the Doctor. 'Between you and me, she's rather an unusual little specimen.'

'Of what?'

The Captain smiled mysteriously at the Doctor's blunt

question. 'That would be telling, old man, wouldn't it? How about yours?'

The Doctor bristled. 'I don't think of Ace as a specimen of anything.'

'Keep your shirt on, old man,' the Captain replied calmly. 'After all, everything's a specimen of something. Even that robot head over there.'

The two men looked towards the excavation as he spoke. Ace and Mags were working away enthusiastically, and the whole of the robot head and neck was now entirely free of the sand. Indeed, the whole top half of its huge body was also in view with the strong articulated metal hands resting on the uncleared soil beneath. The two girls were urged on in their work by the gentle pleading voice: 'Oh, please let me out . . . Please . . . I'll be ever so grateful if you'll let me out . . . Go on, carry on digging . . .'

'What do you reckon, Professor?' Ace called across, stopping her digging for a moment. The Doctor's face was beginning to display signs of alarm. He had been so busy pumping the Captain that he had not really fully considered the significance of the head until now. 'I imagine it was buried for some good reason,' he commented now, his mood suddenly darkening.

'Well, maybe we'll find out what that reason was, eh, Professor?' Ace called back cheerfully. But, before the Doctor could shout any sort of warning, a dramatic change came over the meek and mild robot. Its voice became harsh and threatening. It no longer pleaded but demanded.

'Carry on digging . . . You'll see, I'll show you . . . I'll get my own back on you all . . . See these teeth . . . Look . . .'

Vicious mechanical teeth were displayed inside its gaping mouth, snapping hungrily. The eyes became animated and brightly lit, shooting flame-like rays in all directions. The tea table shattered, causing the tea things to crash to the floor and bringing the Doctor and Captain Cook abruptly to their feet.

'Come on . . . Come here . . . I'll show you . . . I'll show you . . .'

And now the metallic hands were reaching out. Mags was not quick enough to realize her danger. One of the hands snapped shut on her ankle, immobilizing her, while the Doctor and Ace were kept at bay by the rays that shot in all directions.

The Doctor managed to make his way to Mags and helped her extricate her leg from the robot's grip with the aid of his trusty umbrella. But as he struggled, he was aware that Captain Cook was doing nothing for his protégé. Ignoring the Doctor's cries for help, he was still sipping his tea, remarking calmly, 'Remarkable eh, Doctor? Don't often see one like that, do you?'

'I've seen ones like this quite often enough before, thank you,' the Doctor shouted back angrily, as he pulled Mags to safety out of the robot's reach.

'I'll show you . . . I'll teach you . . .'

The robot was still active and still causing chaos with its rays. The Doctor was beginning to wonder how they would ever control it, and kicking himself for not spotting the danger signs earlier.

It was Ace who found the solution. While the Doctor had been rescuing Mags, she had managed to grab the pickaxe she had been excavating with. Now, choosing her moment carefully, so that the robot's eyes were directed elsewhere, she rushed up swiftly behind the head and brought the pickaxe down on it with all her might.

For a moment nothing happened. Then the robot started to seize up. First the arms stopped grabbing. Then the eyes stopped flashing, and the teeth snapping. And finally the voice trailed away into silence.

'I'll get you, I will . . . I'll get you . . . I'll . . . All right, then. Next time perhaps.'

Finally there was silence. Ace, Mags and the Doctor stared down at the fractured and unmoving head.

'Well, well, who'd have thought it? More tea, perhaps?'

Captain Cook, who had done nothing throughout the entire proceedings except drink tea, was holding up the pot. The effrontery of the gesture was so great that even the Doctor was reduced to silence.

'Oi, you – whiteface!'

Despite the earlier mishaps with his bike, Nord the Vandal of the Roads had been making good progress for the last hour. And now he had found the first signs of the Psychic Circus and the Greatest Show in the Galaxy. A clown dressed in bright yellow stood in the sunshine amid the dust-covered wastes practising a tightrope act. Poised apparently precariously on the high wire, the clown looked down blankly at Nord.

'Where's the gig at the Psychic Circus?' Nord demanded fiercely. The clown replied by pointing ahead. There in the distance, Nord saw the Circus for the first time, the striped tent standing out bright and clear against the barren landscape.

Nord urged his motorbike forward. This was what he had come for and he couldn't wait to get there. Nord was not the thoughtful type so he didn't ask himself what he could really expect within that deceptively bright and inviting tent.

Words had been exchanged, angry words on the Doctor's side. Captain Cook had simply refused to accept that he had done anything particularly remiss. He was far more interested in citing other examples, from his vast experience as an explorer, where similar things had happened. When the Doctor tried to stem the flow of reminiscences, the Captain simply beckoned Mags into the jeep, climbed into the driving seat and drove off in a cloud of dust without saying another word.

'Bang goes our lift,' Ace murmured.

'No great loss with that driver, I suspect,' returned the Doctor. 'Come on.'

And so, once again, the duo took to the dust tracks of Segonax, sweltering under its burning sun. At least now they had some idea of what direction they ought to be taking. Assuming, that is, that Captain Cook knew where he was going. That was perhaps a large assumption, but it was best they could manage.

They slogged up the track for an hour or so, not speaking very much and saving their energy for walking. They were just rounding a blind corner, where the track narrowed and an overhanging rock blocked all view of the road ahead, when it happened.

A large black hearse came speeding round the corner. A moment earlier they would both have been killed. But luckily, the Doctor reacted quickly and jumped aside from the road, pulling Ace with him.

The hearse sped on, apparently still oblivious to their presence. But then, Ace supposed as she picked herself up and dusted herself down, they weren't very used to pedestrians on the roads of Segonax.

The Doctor watched the hearse race into the distance and pushed his battered hat back into shape.

'From their driving, you'd think they were trying to drum up some business,' he remarked facetiously.

It was meant as a joke, but then at that moment neither of them had any idea who the occupants of the hearse were.

The stallholder had never known quite such a flow of travellers along her strip of road. The next one looked the most promising: a nice, well scrubbed, neatly dressed young man, with a bright, innocent look behind his large, horn-rimmed glasses, riding on a spick and span new bicycle. It made the stallholder's cynical heart melt just to see him toiling up the road on his bike from the landing base.

'Hi!' The young man got off his bike and modestly introduced himself as the Whizzkid.

'You've no idea what a relief it is to see a nice, clean respectable boy like you, after the riff-raff I usually deal with.' She gestured temptingly towards the fruit and vegetable delights of her stall. 'Can I help you at all?'

'Well, yes,' the Whizzkid announced winningly. 'I was wondering, can you tell me the way to the Psychic Circus?'

The woman's face fell. Her disillusion was total. The Circus's appeal seemed to be irresistible, not only to the rowdy sort of louts you'd expect, but even to ordinary respectable young people. Even after the Whizzkid had purchased some of her fruit for his lunch, she still felt betrayed. She watched him ride off into the distance, vowing never again to put faith in human nature. The truth is that the stallholder had never had any faith in human nature in the first place, but it would have been a brave person who told her that.

As if to add insult to injury, the Whizzkid had barely disappeared from sight when someone else came running up the road towards her. A real hippy this one, shabby and worn out, looking, she mused, just as you're bound to look if you follow that sort of lifestyle and don't eat enough fresh vegetables.

She was not, therefore, particularly impressed when this ragged figure flopped exhausted at her feet. He tried to speak but no words came from his parched throat.

'You can't lie there, you know,' the stallholder insisted.

Then, on this busiest of days, a very smart black car came up the road. The hippy turned and saw it.

'At last,' he managed to murmur almost gratefully. But the stallholder, being who she was, had little interest in finding out what he meant by that remark.

The doors of the limousine opened and a tall white-faced man dressed in undertaker's clothes stepped out, followed by three similarly dressed assistants. 'Is there no end to you weirdos?' the stallholder demanded of the newcomers, but they paid no heed to her question. Instead, they went straight to the sprawling hippy and pulled him brutally to his feet.

'Where's the girl, Bellboy?' the leader demanded.

A look of hope came into Bellboy's eyes. 'She should have reached there by now.'

'If she has, she'll regret it.' The reply was short and brutal as Bellboy, unprotesting now, was dragged into the hearse.

The doors banged shut and it sped off, much to the stallholder's relief. She had had more than enough riff-raff for one day. It's doubtful whether she'd have felt any sympathy for Bellboy even if she'd known how vain his hopes were.

4

The Hippy Bus

'Oh no, I don't believe it.'

The Doctor and Ace were standing at the top of a steep slope, looking down into the dusty valley below. They could make out the outlines of a stranded half-buried bus painted all the colours of the rainbow. But that was not what had caused Ace's remark. It was the sight of the two figures who were in the process of examining the bus, and more particularly the booming voice of the male figure which floated up to them.

'Well, of course, if you've been on as many trips as I have, you get to know these vehicular shrines, and I can tell here that . . .'

Ace looked questioningly at the Doctor. 'Well,' he remarked philosophically, 'at least the bus looks interesting.' Without further ado, they started scrambling down the slope towards the bus. And, of course, towards Captain Cook.

There was one thing that could be said in the Captain's favour. On the surface, at least, he did not appear to bear any grudges. He greeted them like long lost friends, as if nothing had happened. Before very long, he was taking them on a tour of the site rather as if he owned it. It was, even the Doctor had to agree, a site worth examining, particularly the rather crude paintings and scribbles all over the outside of the bus.

'It's obviously some sort of shrine,' the Captain announced. 'I saw one much like this on Dioscuros once.'

The Doctor stopped thoughtfully in his examination in

order to reply. 'Shrine or not,' he returned gravely, 'I can't help feeling there's something sinister here.'

'I wonder that you manage to explore anything, old chap,' Captain Cook mockingly replied. 'Everything seems to alarm you.'

'Not everything,' the Doctor corrected. 'But I trust my instincts.' He fixed the Captain's sceptical eyes. 'As you may recall, they are not always wrong.'

But, fortunately perhaps, before they could get into any further recrimination over the affair of the robot's head, Ace had come up to them. 'Oh, come on, Professor,' she urged impatiently. 'Let's explore.'

The Captain smirked. 'I agree with your young "friend", Doctor. Let's explore.'

Since the Doctor was hardly likely to let himself miss out on anything new and intriguing, whatever his forebodings, all four of them made their way into the bus.

It was cramped inside, with barely enough room for all four of them. And because of the sun beating down on the roof, the atmosphere was stifling. The contents were covered in dust but it was still possible to identify many of them: bright beads, exotic hangings, brass statues, the sort of thing Ace associated with the horrors of those 'Swinging Sixties' her Aunt Rosemary had always gone on about. The Beatles, Aunt Rosemary used to say. You must have heard of them. And Mary Quant, and Carnaby Street. And the love-ins. And flared trousers and the miniskirt . . . come to think of it, Ace mused, Aunt Rosemary on the glories of her misspent youth sounded a bit like Captain Cook's accounts of his favourite expeditions.

Still, there was certainly plenty to explore here, and the Doctor, in particular, was eagerly blowing the dust off objects and examining them more closely.

None of them noticed the curtained-off area at the far end of the bus until the beaded curtain was pulled aside by a powerful mechanical hand.

'Any more fares, please? . . . Any more fares? . . .'

41

All four of them froze in horror. What had emerged was a large and powerful robot, whose intentions were clearly less than friendly. And, for Ace at least, the feature that made the robot particularly alarming was the fact that it was dressed in the garb of a London Buses ticket collector, complete with a ticket machine round its neck.

'Plenty of room on top . . . No standing inside . . .'

The voice was mechanical but precise. It was somebody's cruel idea of a joke, no doubt, to guard a bus with a murderous robotic bus conductor. At least it seemed fairly safe to assume that the robot was murderous, as it advanced towards Captain Cook, who stood nearest, with metallic arms raised as if to strangle him.

'Hold tight please . . . Hold tight . . .'

The Captain backed away but the constraints of the space made this difficult. 'Now, now, old chap,' he mumbled as placatingly as he could. 'Steady on.'

'Fares please . . . Hold on tight . . . Ding ding! . . .'

The robot bus conductor continued to advance on them, before the Captain had his bright idea. 'You've got it wrong, old boy,' he insisted, pointing to the Doctor. 'He's paying the fares, not me.'

And, to Ace's outrage, he managed to scramble out of the bus as the conductor turned its grisly attention, as instructed, towards the Doctor.

'He can't do that,' Ace insisted hotly from her corner of the bus.

'He just has,' Mags returned from hers in a resigned voice.

'Any more fares? . . . Ding ding! . . .'

The Doctor held his ground but then, as he was wedged against one of the bus walls, he did not have a lot of choice. His brain was racing through various possibilities, all too aware that it would have to be very quick if he was to come out of this scrape alive. Then, just as the bus conductor raised its arms to take the Doctor's neck in their powerful grip, the Doctor started to speak, in a sudden incessant flow of words.

'Well, yes, as a matter of fact, I would like a ticket, actually. I'd like a there and back, off-peak, weekend break, supersaver, senior citizen, bi-monthly season with optional luggage facilities and a free cup of coffee in a plastic cup, and make it snappy, you metallic moron . . .'

The conductor stopped dead in its tracks. The flow of words had completely baffled its prefabricated brain. That was the moment the Doctor used to seize hold of the ticket machine and look over its controls.

'If I might take a look . . . Ah yes, I see . . .'

The Doctor pressed one of the buttons on the ticket machine very firmly. There was a fractional pause while the robot vaguely sensed something was wrong, then there was a minor explosion like a car backfiring, and the conductor toppled over inoperative, its metal head bouncing off into a far corner.

The Doctor surveyed the wreckage and grinned at the two girls. 'Just the ticket,' he pronounced.

The post-mortem after this escape was more heated, mainly because Ace got really angry with the Captain about fingering the Doctor in this way. Not helping him was one thing, but actually putting him in mortal danger was another. The upshot, however, was exactly the same as before: Captain Cook silently gestured Mags into the jeep, got into the driving seat and drove off again, leaving the Doctor and Ace high and dry.

'Some people just can't bear to be proved wrong, I suppose,' the Doctor sighed philosophically as he and Ace stood by the stranded bus, watching their chances of a lift recede for a second time.

'He'd have let tin-head do you in,' Ace angrily insisted.

'Let us not bear grudges, Ace,' the Doctor chided her. 'After all, he can't help being a pompous, selfish, self-satisfied meddler.'

'Mags might be OK if he wasn't around,' Ace put in.

'Yes, indeed,' the Doctor agreed, 'if a little odd.' It was the first time they had both considered the precise nature of Mags' oddity. The Captain's little hints had told them nothing. There was, however, in the laconic Mags, fierce and yet biddable, with her animal-like movements and instinctive responses, a mystery they had not yet fathomed.

'Hey, look!' Ace's discovery brought an end to their private musings. There, half hidden in the sand, was something metallic. It was an earring of sharp-edged angular design, hand-made by the look of it.

'You like that?' the Doctor enquired, as Ace held it up admiringly. She nodded enthusiastically. 'Well,' he smiled, 'if there's no keeper then the finder can have it.'

'Ace!' Ace pinned it in a prominent position of her jacket amid all the other badges that clustered there. 'What do you reckon happened here, Professor?' she asked thoughtfully, her anger having melted away. 'Were the people in this bus attacked on their way to the Circus?'

'Presumably,' the Doctor replied with that vagueness which always made Ace suspicious. Sometimes it meant genuine doubt, sometimes it meant he knew something that he wasn't telling her. 'I suppose whatever attacked them destroyed them and wrecked their bus.'

'So the evil you felt,' Ace insisted, 'was that the bus conductor?'

'Yes, I think so,' the Doctor continued vaguely. 'Anyway, whoever left him on guard seems to have gone now. Perhaps they went millennia ago.'

'So it's got nothing to do with the Circus being scary?'

'I'm afraid I think not,' the Doctor smiled, studying her reactions closely. 'That was all just good publicity.'

'Pity,' Ace returned, meeting his questioning eyes. 'Might have made the Circus more interesting.' She paused. 'Are we still going there?'

'Oh yes,' the Doctor answered enthusiastically. 'I feel in

44

just the right mood. And, after two brushes with death in one day, I rather hoped you might be too.'

'If you say so, Doctor.' Ace followed him away from the hippy bus without much enthusiasm.

'Doctor, eh?' the Doctor exclaimed in pleased surprise. 'So you can remember to call me Doctor if you want to.'

Ace nodded cheerfully. 'Seems so, Professor.'

The Doctor rolled his eyes in mock despair. They started walking up the road, once again in the steps of Captain Cook. But when Ace thought over that conversation in the light of later events, she did wonder if the Doctor really did know what they were letting themselves in for at the Psychic Circus.

The undertaker's clothes slid from the leader's body. There was nothing incongruous now about his appearance. The white face and the red gash of a mouth were at one with the spangled black and white of his glittering, broad-shouldered clown's costume with the silver sequinned snake coiling its way around his body. The Chief Clown was in his element in another way too, for now he was standing in the vestibule of the Psychic Circus.

Kneeling before him was Bellboy, quivering and cowed, his face even more lined and ashen, although a flicker of defiance still lingered. He whimpered occasionally but otherwise was silent, as were the two assistant clowns who had brutally dragged him there.

'Isn't it enough that we've got him back?' The speaker was a woman of maybe thirty, wearing a kaftan and multi-coloured beads, on her head a scarf, in her ears large circular earrings, the very picture of a fortune-teller or palmist. She was the only one of the group clustered round the prone Bellboy who appeared to be showing any concern for his state.

'You know it isn't enough just to recapture him. Morgana,' the Chief Clown snapped back brutally. 'He must be punished.'

'Flowerchild . . . Flowerchild . . .'

Bellboy's whimperings had finally found a voice. The Chief Clown smiled but it was not a kind or mirthful smile. 'Poor Bellboy,' he sneered. 'He still thinks she may have escaped.'

'Listen, Bellboy . . .' Morgana was bending down now to try and explain as gently as she could to Bellboy what had happened, and was going to happen. But the Chief Clown would have none of it.

'Save your breath, Morgana.' He turned to the attendant clowns. Over the loudspeakers in the vestibule came the anticipatory roar of a crowd waiting in the ring. 'Take Bellboy into the ring,' he commanded. 'He knows what's waiting there.'

'Please, no . . . no.' The command galvanized Bellboy into one last plea for his punishment to be averted. He knew what it was and he dreaded it, but there was no reprieve. In his ears the roar of the crowd grew louder and louder as he was dragged away from the vestibule through the entrance tunnel towards the ring.

'What if a visitor arrives now?' Morgana demanded anxiously once he was gone.

The Chief Clown smiled and shrugged. 'If they come, they come.'

A clown in green was practising on stilts in the blazing sunlight. It was the first indication to Mags and the Captain that their search was nearly over. Guided by a friendly wave and gesture from the clown, they drove on and saw the Circus lying before them.

Eagerly, they parked the jeep nearby and strode quickly towards the tent, lifted the tent flap, and found themselves in some sort of vestibule facing a woman dressed like a fortune-teller. She seemed a little on edge to Mags but Captain Cook had no time for such suspicions.

'Greetings, my good woman,' he boomed. 'This is the Psychic Circus, isn't it?'

46

'Yes, that's right.' And from over the loudspeakers came roars of approving laughter. The audience in the big tent was clearly enjoying the show.

'Sounds like things are going well,' beamed the Captain. 'Come on, Mags.'

'But . . .'

'But what?'

'You can't go in just now, you see,' the woman explained. 'There's a speciality act being rehearsed and . . .'

'All the better.' Captain Cook would hear no excuses. He was a seasoned explorer and was not easily fobbed off with feeble protests. He swept towards the entrance tunnel, beckoning Mags to follow.

'You don't understand. You shouldn't. . .'

The woman's voice stopped. A tall clown dressed in white, black and silver had appeared in the tunnel, a welcoming smile on his face. His appearance startled even Mags and the Captain, but the clown kept on smiling and, stepping aside, gestured them towards the ring.

The Captain thanked him grandly and walked on with Mags in his wake. As they got nearer to their goal, to the long promised Psychic Circus, over the roar of the crowd they could hear a voice declaiming in a soft but penetrating voice to an equally soft but insistent beat.

'So welcome, folks, I'm so glad you all came

To one big circus with one big famous name.

There's lots of surprises you can take it from me

At the Greatest Show in the Galaxy . . .'

And Mags knew instinctively, even before they reached the ring, that in coming here they had made the most terrible mistake.

5

The Psychic Circus

The red clown who was practising some very complex tumbling routine nodded encouragingly and gestured them on. They were indeed nearing the Psychic Circus. An end to trudging along the dusty lanes of Segonax was at hand and their aching feet could finally have the weight taken off them.

'Not as far as we feared,' the Doctor announced cheerfully, returning the red clown's friendly wave.

Ace looked up at the clown's fixed smile and gave a little inner shudder. 'I still think clowns are creepy,' she insisted.

'Nonsense.' The Doctor was already striding eagerly towards the circus tent that stood out clearly in its bright primary colours amid the yellow wastes around. Still less than enthusiastic, Ace trailed behind him.

As they approached, the laughter and applause from the circus became more and more distinct. At least it sounds as if someone's having a good time, Ace thought.

And then she heard it. Faintly, very faintly, someone was screaming, and screaming in terror. The laughter and clapping almost blotted it out, but not quite, not if you really listened. It must be something really scary to upset somebody that much, Ace decided.

She stopped. 'Don't you hear it, Professor?'

'Hear what?'

'That screaming.' The Doctor stopped to listen, but apparently he could hear nothing unususal. Ace strained her ears again, and realized that she could no longer hear the screaming either, only delighted crowd noises, almost as if the screaming had been turned off abruptly.

'I was sure I heard . . .' Her voice trailed away and the Doctor grinned. 'I think you're just making excuses, Ace, because you don't like circuses.'

'No, no, it's not that.' Ace indignantly insisted. But however hard she listened, she couldn't hear the least sound of someone screaming above the jollification. The Doctor was already moving towards the tent. Unless she was to be branded a coward, Ace had no choice but to follow him.

A tall clown in white, black and silver appeared at the entrance to the tent, beckoning them in welcomingly. The sight of him again made Ace stop in her tracks. The Doctor, who was almost at the entrance, turned back to her.

'Well, are we going in or aren't we?'

The clown gestured again, and Ace followed the Doctor without another word. Perhaps she had imagined the screaming. In her heart of hearts, she did not believe that, but if the Doctor wanted her to go in, then go in she must.

In the circus vestibule was a ticket booth, and on its ledge a crystal ball. And behind that a woman, not unfriendly, who apparently doubled as ticket collector and fortune-teller. Around the canvas walls of this entrance lay posters and other mementos of past triumphs.

'Welcome, one and all, to the Psychic Circus!' A tinny fanfare accompanied the woman's welcome. Ace almost left in disgust but was at least relieved to see that the tall clown was not present. Busy in the ring, she supposed.

Perhaps her disgust was less well hidden than she supposed, because she heard the Doctor apologizing for her as he introduced the two of them.

The woman, who presented herself as Morgana, was all too understanding of Ace's bad mood, rather to Ace's annoyance. 'It's no problem,' she insisted in her casual, laid-back way. 'All of us here believe in letting our feelings hang out. There's no point in getting uptight, now is there?'

Ace did not believe her ears. She'd only heard talk like that once before, when Aunt Rosemary talked about the love-ins in the swinging Sixties or the swing-ins in the loving Sixties or whatever it was. She hadn't come half-way across the galaxy to hear people spouting that old stuff. However, she wisely kept her thoughts to herself and left it to the Doctor to be charming to Morgana.

'That is, of course, the reason why we got into circuses in the first place,' Morgana was now explaining.

'We?' the Doctor queried.

'The founder members of the Psychic Circus.' The Doctor nodded encouragingly and Morgana continued as the Doctor's roving eyes took in the contents of the vestibule. As well as the posters and reviews there were also some large and impressive kites, all decorated with a rather distinctive eye symbol. That was a nice touch, he thought.

Morgana was still talking about the founder members. 'We were all really into personal expression, you see,' she was explaining. 'The circus gave us all a chance to express ourselves by developing our individual skills.'

'And what's your special skill, if I might enquire?' beamed the Doctor. Morgana pointed to the crystal ball. 'Fortune telling, of course.' She moved closer to the Doctor. 'Would you like to see the future?'

The Doctor's face clouded suddenly. 'Not just yet,' he answered in a rather strained voice, before pulling himself together and continuing. 'The Psychic Circus has grown into quite a sizeable little operation by the look of it.'

'The Greatest Show in the Galaxy,' Morgana returned proudly.

'Just so,' the Doctor agreed. His eyes scanned the posters. 'My, my, you have got around, haven't you? Marpesia. Othrys. Eudamus. Even the Grand Pagoda on Cinethon.'

Morgana nodded nostalgically. 'Yes, we used to have great times back in the old days, going from planet to planet. But we've really got settled in here since . . .' She stopped herself abruptly.

'Since?' The Doctor was all alert, but the moment had passed and Morgana retreated once more into blander generalities. 'After all,' she sighed wistfully, 'you have to hang up your travelling shoes and stop wandering sooner or later, don't you?'

'So I've been told,' the Doctor replied. 'Personally I've just kept on wandering.'

'Will you please take your seats . . .'

A summons to the ring issued from the loudspeakers, momentarily cutting across the excited babble of the crowd that had filled their ears since they'd entered the vestibule. Ace looked questioningly at the Doctor, her reluctance still visible to Morgana as well as to the Doctor.

'Are you sure you want to go in?' Morgana demanded, a furtive look coming into her eyes.

'That is why we're here,' the Doctor replied drily.

Morgana took a deep breath and made a decision. 'Look,' she began. 'I don't know how to put this but I've taken a fancy to you and . . .'

What she was going to say or to warn them about they never discovered. For at that moment the tall Chief Clown reappeared at the entrance to the circus. Morgana immediately changed tone and went back into her previous routine, assuring them that, of course, they were free to go and 'do their own thing.'

'We don't have to buy tickets then?' the Doctor enquired.

'Tickets?' Morgana returned blankly. 'What for?'

'To go in.'

'You're in already,' the Chief Clown cut in, making one of his flamboyant welcoming gestures. Behind him the roar of the crowd rose once more as if in support of his invitation. 'This way please.' He lifted the flap of the entrance to the ring.

'Please make your way to the Big Top now . . .' the loudspeakers blared.

'One moment . . .' Morgana again seemed on the point of stopping them entering, but she caught the eye of the Chief Clown and once more changed tack. 'I – I just wanted to say – I hope you both enjoy the performance.'

'Thank you.' The Doctor smiled at Morgana who had retreated to the contemplation of her crystal ball, and then passed under the flap held for him by the Chief Clown. Ace followed him, reluctantly enduring the cold scrutiny of the Chief Clown. Did he give a start of recognition when he noticed the earring she had found by the bus pinned there among her other badges? Or was she imagining things again? She did not feel very sure of anything at that moment.

Ace pursued the Doctor swiftly into the tent tunnel that led from the vestibule into the Big Top. The walls were made of strips of light canvas fabric that billowed with the force of unseen winds. There was something both oppressive and insubstantial about them. The multi-coloured lights trained through the walls gave enough light to see by, but also added to the oppression with their strange shaped and oddly coloured shadows. In this context, the roar of the crowd in the Big Top ahead was almost comforting.

The Doctor finally pulled back the flap of the Big Top itself and Ace breathed a sigh of relief, but only for a second. It hit them both with bitter force that everything was almost pitch black. And, oddly, there was no longer any cheering. They were stranded without an usherette or anyone to guide them in a vast black silent space.

'Maybe we've arrived between performances,' the Doctor suggested. 'Let's see if we can find a seat until things get under way.'

They tentatively edged their way into the blackness. They could see up to a few feet in front of them but that did not prevent them from bumping shins and tripping over uneven wooden planks in the floor.

'Over here.' The Doctor had finally located a row of

seats. Curiously, given that they were probably completely alone, they still found themselves speaking in subdued tones.

'In a moment our eyes'll get used to the dark,' the Doctor whispered once they were both settled.

'Assuming there's anything worth seeing,' Ace grumbled.

'Just a moment. Listen.' They both held their breath and listened. Behind them they heard the sound of rustling papers and then voices – a little girl's first.

'Daddy, daddy . . .'

'What?'

'I want an ice-cream.'

'You've already had one.'

'But, Daddy . . .'

'I've told you once and I'm not telling you again. Shut up and eat your popcorn.'

Now they were becoming more used to the dark, Ace and the Doctor could just about make out the speakers, only two rows behind them. There were three of them, a mother, a father and a little girl. They were really the most ordinary looking family Ace had ever seen, so ordinary it would have been difficult to find anything very distinctive about any of them. The only odd thing was finding them here in a darkened circus tent munching away at their snacks.

'We are not alone, Ace.'

'Not quite,' Ace agreed. 'But it looks like it's just us and them.' Her eyes scanned the rest of the seating as best they could. It all appeared empty. 'What a con! I mean, where's Mags and the Captain?'

'Perhaps they've not turned up yet. Who knows?' The Doctor shrugged, taking another look at the family. 'Still, it wouldn't do any harm to see if they know anything.'

Slowly and carefully he made his way through the gloom to where the family sat, listening all the while to their bland exchanges.

'Well, they should be starting up again soon,' the mother remarked flatly. 'Have a crisp, father.'

53

'Greetings.' The Doctor popped up behind the family, a friendly grin on his face. There was no response but he ploughed on regardless. 'Not many in today, I see. Are you regulars or is this your first visit too? Let me introduce myself . . .'

There was still no reply. The family simply munched on, but now the mother extended the bag of crisps to the Doctor. 'Oh, er, thank you very much.' It seemed politic to take one of the proffered crisps and eat it, even though it looked and tasted foul. 'Mmm, delicious,' the Doctor lied. 'Now, I was just wondering if . . .'

He could probably have talked to the family until he was blue in the face without getting any further acknowledgement of his presence. Fortunately, however, the circus music started up and Ace called him back to his seat. The circus was about to begin. 'It's been lovely talking to you,' the Doctor lied again as he hurried back. Then all of them, mother, father, daughter, the Doctor and Ace settled back to watch the show.

Light flooded into the ring. The music grew louder, then a line of white-faced clowns appeared, cartwheeling and somersaulting and stilt-walking and juggling. Everything was quite extraordinarily skilled and precise, Ace thought, but rather creepy and unreal because of that.

The Doctor, however, was more taken by something else. As the light spread over the whole of the ring, it revealed, placed evenly around the edge, four large weather-beaten stones.

'Do you see those memorial stones, Ace?' The Doctor pointed them out to Ace and she saw they were covered in what looked like prehistoric inscriptions. 'Remarkable,' the Doctor observed, but he did not have a chance to investigate further; the Ringmaster had entered the ring.

An imposing figure, whip in hand, he stood confidently there in the spotlight, welcoming them with a cool smile and a polished speech delivered to a half-heard musical beat.

'Now welcome, folks, and I mean that from the heart,
The Greatest Show is just about to start.
It's happening right here before your very eyes
And I can assure you, you're in for a surprise.
But then nothing's quite as it seems to be
In the Greatest Show in the Galaxy.'

He beckoned one of the clowns to his side with a knowing smile. The clown approached obediently and then the Ringmaster turned him round and pressed a lever. The clown's back sprang open. The Ringmaster pointed mockingly inside. Robots, Ace gasped, the clowns are all robots. No wonder they're so well drilled. The discovery made her no more comfortable to be there but the Doctor was still giving every sign of enjoying the show so she kept her feelings to herself.

His point made, the Ringmaster snapped shut the robotic mechanism and immediately the clown cartwheeled away to join his other robotic brethren. The Ringmaster clicked his fingers authoritatively and a ghostly drum-roll boomed out.

As he began to speak once more, the Ringmaster's eyes scanned the whole tent, building up a sense of tremendous anticipation.

'Now listen, folks, we've a great new act.
He's a real find and that's a fact.
He'll entertain you and he'll make you stare
And our great new act is seated over there.'

The spot swivelled round the tent and picked out the Doctor. The Doctor rose in surprise but there could be no doubt that he was the person intended. Canned applause from the loudspeakers system acclaimed the choice.

'Come on, Doctor, don't be shy,' the Ringmaster insisted, beckoning him to enter the ring.

'I'm not entirely sure that I really should,' the Doctor said, not moving from his seat.

'No false modesty, Doctor, we know you're good,' grinned the Ringmaster.

'This is most unexpected. Are you sure you want me?'

'There's no mistake, Doctor, come on in, just feel free.'

Ace tugged urgently at the Doctor's sleeve. Every instinct in her body told her there was danger here. 'Don't go, Professor,' she pleaded.

'What harm can it do?' The Doctor turned a calm face to her. Was she worrying unduly? The Doctor usually knew what he was doing. Didn't he?

'Exactly, Doctor,' the Ringmaster gleamed. 'But the decision is up to you.'

To Ace's horror, the Doctor made his decision. To an ever-growing volume of canned applause, he left his seat and went smiling into the ring. Ace could not believe it. Was he mad? He had told her he loved circuses and admired the acts, but was he really so infatuated with them not to notice the danger signs?

The family munched impassively on. Ace stood, uncertain what to do and then, galvanized into action, ran after him. A group of robot clowns gathered to greet her but the circle they formed around her was not just to welcome her, she realized. It was to prevent her from reaching the Doctor.

'Well, you certainly don't waste any time, do you?' she could hear him remarking to the Ringmaster. 'I had intended to see what the competition was up to before putting myself forward for the talent contest but since you insist . . .'

'Indeed, we do,' the Ringmaster agreed smoothly. 'And no doubt you'll want to get yourself prepared. Let me show you and your charming assistant to the dressing room.'

'Lead on.' And, before Ace could reach him, the Doctor had disappeared through the performers' entrance into the backstage area. When he was gone, the atmosphere was suddenly different, and uglier. The Chief Clown's face appeared above that of the robotic clowns, sinister and questioning. Ace wanted to evade him but the encircling clowns held her trapped.

'Where did you find that?' The Chief Clown pointed to the earring Ace had found. She had not been wrong about his interest earlier then, she thought.

'Are you a robot too?' Ace returned insolently to show she was not intimidated.

'No. I'm not,' the Chief Clown answered in his silky voice.

'Pity.' Ace was trying to calculate a way of escape now. She had located the nearest exit and if she could only dodge between the two clowns who blocked her way through to it . . .

The Chief Clown came nearer. 'So tell me where you found it,' he insisted. The Doctor was out of earshot now and Ace was on her own. She made a sudden decision. Ducking as low as she could, she pushed her way beneath the linked arms of the two nearest clowns and ran for the exit.

'After her!' she heard the Chief Clown calling as she tore with all her might along the billowing dark tunnel with its eerie shadows and unexplained noises. She had no doubt now of the Chief Clown's ill intentions and for the moment she would have to concentrate on her own survival. The Doctor would have to look after himself.

'Just over there, Doctor.' They were backstage now and the Ringmaster was indicating where he should go to prepare himself.

'Where's Ace?' The Doctor was suddenly aware that she was not behind him. He had been sure she would follow. 'I can't go on until she's . . .'

And then he heard an all too familiar booming voice:

'Of course, on the Planet Iphitus the Galvanic Catastrophods are not what they were, but they're still worth a look if you're doing a tour of the Southern Nebula and have an aeon or two to spare . . .'

The Captain looked up as the Doctor approached and smiled amicably in recognition. He was sitting in an area marked off by distinctive canvas curtains, taking tea. Mags was with him but silent and watchful as ever. The unlucky recipient of the Captain's flood of reminiscences, however, was none other than Nord, the Vandal of the Roads. He was eating a vast meat-filled sandwich and the Doctor was not surprised to notice that he was clearly finding Captain Cook's chat less than riveting.

'Captain Cook, I presume.' The words sounded oddly familiar to the Doctor as he spoke them, but he could not recall in which existence he had heard them. 'So you have arrived after all, Captain.'

'Of course,' the Captain returned heartily. 'Come and join us, Doctor. It's one big happy family, eh, Nord?'

'Yeah,' the Vandal of the Roads returned sourly, biting deep into his disgusting sandwich. 'Except when you're gassing on.'

'Well, I'm not sure . . .' The Doctor hesitated. Ace had still not reappeared behind him and instead the clowns had gathered in a group that had a distinctly ominous feel to it.

'Nonsense, old man,' the Captain insisted. 'We're having a ball here.' He gestured to Mags to produce a stool for the Doctor while he himself deigned to pour a cup of tea for him. It certainly looked perfectly harmless, and the Doctor felt he could do with some light refreshment before he went back into the ring.

With a shrug, he walked into the canvas room and took the offered stool and cup of tea. 'There we are, old man,' the Captain said solicitously. 'Comfy?'

The Doctor was going to reply that he was very comfy, thank you, but he was still worried about what had happened to Ace. Unfortunately, he didn't have a chance to say a word on either subject because behind him a grille dropped across the doorway, and a moment later the attendant clowns pulled back the canvas curtains to reveal iron bars. Captain Cook and his tea-party were not in a waiting room at all; they were shut in a cage.

'Anything the matter, old chap?' the Captain enquired casually, regarding the Doctor's startled features.

'But this is a trap,' the Doctor said in disbelief, taking in the full horror of his situation. 'I've fallen into a trap. Stupid complacent fool that I am, I've fallen for it.'

'Yes, I know, old man,' Captain Cook agreed without the least show of remorse or surprise. 'Never mind, have some tea. I was in a very similar situation once you know, when I was exploring the Granite Caves of Veturia.'

The Doctor sat in mortified shame. Nord ate on hungrily. Mags slunk back as if ashamed of the deception she had aided. The Captain, however, simply sipped his tea.

'Why?'

'Why what, old man?'

'Why let me be trapped? It's so pointless. I could have saved you and Mags.'

The Captain shook his head pityingly. 'I wouldn't be too sure about that, Doctor. These circus chappies are pretty smart customers, for all their "letting it all hang out" mumbo-jumbo.'

Mags rose to her feet and paced restlessly about. 'Maybe we could have got away,' she burst out. 'If we'd made a break for it there and then at the start. If only you'd . . .'

'Now, now, Mags,' the Captain replied soothingly, 'no use getting upset. And that is an order.'

Mags subsided as quickly as she had erupted. Whatever the hold Captain Cook had over this strange girl, the Doctor noted, it was certainly a powerful one. Despairing of any true explanation from the Captain, he turned instead to the chomping Nord. 'How about you?' he enquired politely. 'Why didn't you speak out?' But Nord turned away with a disgusted grunt. There was no enlightenment there either.

'Save your energy, Doctor,' the Captain advised. 'You'll soon see why.' He paused to sip more tea. 'I think you'll find that all of us in here have developed a survival philosophy. Which is why we welcomed you in. The more the merrier really.'

The Doctor stared at him. 'So what is happening here then? Is some sort of talent contest going on or not?'

The Captain pondered this judiciously. 'Well, yes, I suppose so. But in a way it's more like a survival of the fittest.'

A strange shuffling noise distracted the Doctor from pursuing this further. A new figure had appeared outside the cage. His age was impossible to guess, his face wasted and hollow, his once colourful clothes tattered and dirty apart from a large gleaming medallion he wore round his neck. The overriding impression was of mental vacuity and physical feebleness but the Doctor could not help feeling that it had not always been thus.

The newcomer grinned feebly at them all and waved the broom that he carried. 'That's Deadbeat,' the Captain explained. 'He does odd jobs about the place. I wouldn't bother about it too much though. The fellow's mind is completely gone.

Deadbeat noticed the Doctor's gaze upon him. The large vacant eyes stared unseeingly into the Doctor's. And then Deadbeat gave a mad empty grin and held his broom like a guitar. He started to sing in a rambling, near tuneless way but the words made little or no sense.

'Gone, gone,' Deadbeat droned. 'All really gone . . . All really gone down the road.' Still singing his bizarre ditty, he started to sweep the floor outside the cage.

But there was something about his sweeping and his singing that got through to Nord. Leaping up from his stool, sending fragments of his disgusting sandwich off in all directions, the Vandal of the Roads shouted angrily at the sweeper, 'Clear off! I hate you. I hate all your kind. I'm Nord, see. The toughest Infernal Extraterrestrial there is.' His angry eyes met Deadbeat's vacant ones. 'See?' he demanded.

But Deadbeat only cackled madly in his face and,

returning to his sweeping, soon moved out of sight to work on other parts of the circus.

'What a fool I've been.' The Doctor sat desolately contemplating the folly of not listening to Ace. He knew there was something here in the Psychic Circus he had to find and had to confront but this was not the way to do it, walking straight into the first simple trap somebody chose to set for him.

'Frankly, old man, I have to agree,' the Captain returned, amiably adding to the heap of coals the Doctor had laid on his own head. 'Number one rule of the inter-galactic explorer, Doctor. If you hear somebody talking about good vibes and letting it all hang out, run a mile.'

'We didn't,' Mags objected angrily, but the Captain chose to ignore her interruption. Instead he studied the Doctor benignly while the Doctor turned his attention to the ring that lay behind a curtain just a matter of yards from their cage.

'What happens in there?' the Doctor asked.

'In where?'

'In the Big Top.' The Doctor paused. 'During the talent contest.'

'Oh, something pretty nasty, I should imagine,' Captain Cook answered, draining his tea.

'Next contestant ready please . . .' Over the loudspeakers came a voice that the Doctor now recognized as that of the Ringmaster.

On hearing the words, the Captain put down his teacup, rose nonchalantly and walked towards Nord. He pulled out a coin from his pocket. 'Remember our agreement, Nord?' Nord nodded curtly.

'Heads or tails?' The coin was poised now on the Captain's tensed thumb. Nord studied it intently. The whole cage was silently watching the exchange between the two men.

Nord gulped. 'Tails,' he decided. The Captain tossed the

coin. It fell to the ground and the two men bent over to examine it.

'Heads,' the Captain announced coolly.

'So?'

'So you're on next, Nord.' Nord's response to this decision was immediate and brutal. He grabbed the Captain angrily by the throat. 'What did you say?'

The Captain kept his calm. 'We all agreed. Didn't we, Mags?' And, as he spoke her name, Mags rushed to his aid, leaping on Nord's powerful back and pulling him away from the Captain's throat. The outcome of the fierce scuffle would nevertheless have been in doubt if, at that moment, the door had not lifted to admit the Chief Clown and his henchmen.

'Next contestant over there.' The robot clowns prised the struggling Nord away from the Captain and Mags. 'Get him ready,' the Chief Clown commanded. And, in a scene that would have been ludicrous if the outcome was not likely to be so grim, the attendant clowns prepared Nord for the ring. Some clowns applied stage make-up. Others arranged and laquered his hair. Finally he was forced into a skimpy leopard skin of the type worn by circus strongmen.

'You were lucky, Captain,' the Doctor remarked while this was going on.

'Not really,' the Captain returned, grinning. He held up the coin he had used. It double headed. 'I got a whole set of these useful little knick-knacks when I was on the planet Leophantos. Swapped them with some bug-eyed monster for a supersonic pencil sharpener.' He seated himself once again. 'Like I said, Doctor, it's every man for himself here.'

He smiled genially. In the meantime, Nord's preparation was over and the new style Vandal of the Roads was ready for his debut. Despite his strength, his unwillingness to make his historic entry into the ring presented no problem. The robot clowns held and controlled him as if he were nothing but a tiny fly caught in a large spider's web. Cowed and silent now, he was bundled off under the Chief Clown's orders to meet his fate – whatever, the Doctor thought grimly, that might be.

One of the departing clowns handed the Doctor a set of Indian clubs. He stared at the gift in some perplexity. 'What am I supposed to do with these?' he asked of no one in particular.

'Practice juggling I imagine,' the Captain replied. 'Your chances of survival in the ring are better, of course, if you keep them entertained.'

'They let you out again?'

'No, old man,' Captain Cook continued imperturbably. 'But you last longer.'

Looking into the Captain's eyes at that moment, the Doctor realized they were the most ruthless he had ever seen in all his travels through the galaxy.

6

Nord's Finest Hour

Ace cautiously emerged from her hiding place. It looked as if her strategy had worked. Hidden behind the billowing walls, she had heard the robot clowns run past. Her new earring had already proved its usefulness, its sharp edge cutting a slit in the walls for her to slip through and out of her pursuers' way. But she was not taking any chances. She kept stealthily to the shadows as she edged along the entrance tunnel towards the vestibule.

Morgana was still there staring intently into her crystal ball. Morgana who had, Ace believed, tried to warn them and been scared off by the arrival of the Chief Clown. Perhaps now, while she was alone, Ace could approach her and beg her to tell everything she knew. It was a risk, of course, but Ace rather liked risks.

Before Ace could attract Morgana's attention, however, she heard footsteps approaching. Swiftly Ace slid behind one of the large kites that were stacked round the vestibule. Still, if she could not question Morgana, at least she might learn something about what was going on from an over-heard conversation. With any luck she would be near enough to hear every word, and the kite large enough to cover her completely.

The new arrival was the Ringmaster. Morgana had clearly summoned him. 'We have to talk,' she insisted urgently.

'Well?' Ace strained forward to listen. She could hear Morgana turning pages. The pages, no doubt, that listed the arrivals at the Psychic Circus.

'Look at all those names,' Morgana began, her voice wracked with unhappiness. 'Does that make you feel good? It wasn't always like this, was it? Not before we came to this dreadful place. We used to have fun. We were free spirits then.'

'We are now.' But the Ringmaster's assertion sounded strangely hollow. He did not sound as if he believed it himself. Having only seen him in the full confidence and power of his role in the Big Top, it had not occurred to Ace that he might feel the same anxieties and unhappinesses that were so much more visible in Morgana.

Morgana pressed on, sensing his lack of conviction. 'You think so?' she demanded. 'It feels like we're part of a machine.'

But she had pushed her advantage too far. 'We're not leaving, if that's what you mean,' the Ringmaster returned brusquely.

'We must.' There was something desperate in Morgana's tone now.

'So you keep saying,' the Ringmaster answered impatiently. His voice took on a jeering tone. 'But you haven't gone, have you?'

'I try,' Morgana insisted, 'and then . . .' Her voice trailed away. Even without being able to see her face, Ace could sense the weight of desolation and despair.

The Ringmaster reacted quickly. With the bright, optimistic words he poured out, Ace knew he was trying to convince not just Morgana but himself too. 'Just so long as they keep on coming, Morgana. That's what matters.' His voice became softer, more persuasive, more conspiratorial. 'And they will. No doubt of that. We're a success, don't you understand? An intergalactic success.' There was no reply as he talked on. 'The others couldn't take the pace, that's all. Deadbeat. Bellboy. Flowerchild. The rest. Don't you understand? They wanted to live in the past. The old lazy ways. Not us. We'll make the Psychic Circus known everywhere.'

'Known for what?' There was a wealth of bitterness behind Morgana's challenge.

Then, to Ace's dismay, the Chief Clown entered the vestibule with two attendant clowns. The others disturbed her, but she could understand them, see how and why they felt. The Chief Clown, though, was a cold, terrifying enigma.

'Well?' The Ringmaster turned to greet the newcomer who had stopped uncomfortably close to Ace's hiding place. She hoped against hope that she would not be discovered. Here, she realized, was the whole team responsible for running the Psychic Circus.

'That new pair worry me,' the Chief Clown was saying. 'The girl that escaped had one of Flowerchild's earrings.'

Ace edged closer. Flowerchild! Where was this person now? Had she once been part of the Circus? How many others were there like her?

'Have they found the girl?' the Ringmaster enquired. Ace felt a certain grim satisfaction in knowing that they were discussing her whereabouts when she was only feet away from them.

'She can't have gone far,' the Chief Clown was saying. 'I'm going to search for her myself. Can you manage in the ring without me for a while?'

'Sure,' the Ringmaster growled. 'But make sure you find her.' Without another word, he returned to the ring.

'But what about Bellboy?' Morgana's question obviously stopped the Chief Clown in his tracks. And it must have taken quite a lot of nerve on Morgana's part, given the fear the Chief Clown seemed to inspire in her.

'Let's hope he's learnt his lesson, shall we?' the Chief Clown replied, with a smoothness more frightening than anger would have been. 'We have to make sure he gets back to work. Bellboy made all of these clowns for us. Bellboy can repair them.'

In her excitement at realizing how much she was on the point of understanding about the Circus, Ace involuntarily moved forward. If only she could hear the rest of this conversation and then find the Doctor, she could . . . But her movement was too violent. To her horror the kite fell forward giving off a long bleeping noise. She had triggered some sort of alarm. Worse, she was fully revealed to the gaze of the Chief Clown.

For a moment that for Ace could have lasted a second or an hour, everyone was immobile with surprise. Then, before the others could recover, she bolted quickly towards the nearest exit from the vestibule. A robot clown moved to block her but her momentum was such that she knocked it aside. But, as she disappeared down another of these apparently endless billowing corridors, she knew she had gained only a few seconds. The Chief Clown and his cohorts would not be far behind.

Morgana, left alone once again, replaced the fallen kite with mixed feelings. Most of the time now she felt fatally divided within herself. The tension was becoming unbearable. She knew that she did not have it in her to attempt to escape as Flowerchild and Bellboy had done. But to stay at her booth day after day was almost as impossible.

'Hello, this is the Psychic Circus, isn't it?'

Morgana turned to see an earnest looking youth staring brightly at her through large horn-rimmed spectacles. Not at all their usual sort of customer, she mused, as she assured him that this was, indeed, the Greatest Show in the Galaxy.

The Whizzkid beamed in wide-eyed delight. 'Oh great,' he sighed in pure content. 'I've come half-way across the Southern Nebula to be here. I want to enter the talent contest.' He paused dramatically. 'You see, I know all about the Psychic Circus. In fact, I'm its greatest fan.'

Words for once completely failed Morgana. Was there never to be an end to her torments?

Since she had first known the Doctor, Ace seemed to have spent a lot of her time running down corridors. And the fact that these were billowing canvas corridors seemed to make little difference to the nightmare repetition. Eventually she could run no further and had to stop for breath. She listened intently. Nobody appeared to be following her – yet.

But then she heard a different sound, a low sad moaning. It appeared to be coming from behind a section of the billowing curtains. Then she noticed a closed flap. She took a deep breath and lifted it until she could see what was beyond.

Behind was a small cupboard-like space surrounded by canvas curtains. The space was dark but there was no doubt what the source of the moaning was.

Strapped there against a large kite was a youngish man dressed in a military-style jacket and bell-bottom trousers. But his clothes were faded and torn, and the face, still young and handsome in its way, was lined and wasted. The eyes, too, were weary and the body shook involuntarily in sudden nervous spasms. Most shockingly of all, perhaps, the hair was almost white, as if the man had been through some terrible experience. A horrible accident perhaps, or an electric shock.

The man saw her and mumbled piteously. Ace stared, uncertain what to do. People like this made Ace uncomfortable. She did not like to admit she didn't really know yet how to cope with deep emotion in other people. Nevertheless, pity impelled her to pull the flap shut and move towards him. But she could make no sense of the man's distracted mumblings.

'Look, I want to help,' Ace assured him. 'But you're not making it easy. Can't you at least tell me . . .'

The man only cowered back in terror still more. And then Ace heard why. Someone, the Chief Clown no doubt, was coming down the corridor. Oh great, Ace sarcastically thought to herself. Looking around quickly for somewhere to hide, she realized the only place was right behind the kite that the man was strapped to. She would have to trust that he would not betray her.

'Don't tell on me, will you?' she begged as she concealed herself just in time. The flap was pulled back once more. As she had feared, it was the Chief Clown. Luckily, the Chief Clown seemed to have come to see his prisoner, not to look for Ace.

It was an uncomfortable experience to be in such close proximity to the Chief Clown as he leaned forward and whispered close to the man's face, 'Learnt your lesson, eh, Bellboy? No more running away now?' Bellboy only groaned by way of reply, but the Chief Clown took it as agreement. 'Good. Because we've got some important repair work for you to do. The Conductor's been damaged.'

Ace's mind raced. So this was Bellboy, who had made all the robotic clowns. He had been punished for running away, and he was to repair the Conductor. Was the Conductor the robot that had attacked the Doctor at what she thought of as the hippy bus? And wasn't that where she had found the earring that so interested the Chief Clown? The earring that belonged to, what was the name, Flowerchild?

While she shrank back in her hiding place, attempting to make sense of all this, Bellboy was untied from the kite by two attendant clowns and pulled roughly to his feet. He was in such a feeble state that they had virtually to pick him up and carry him away.

The last to leave was the Chief Clown who gave one last searching glance round the small room. 'That girl must be somewhere,' he murmured to himself.

Then he pulled the flap shut and the girl in question was left in the dark to figure out just what she was going to do next.

Nord's confidence was beginning to come back. After all, they had given him a strong-man's costume, hadn't they? And there was no doubt he was strong, strong enough to do any feats this collection of white-faced wimps were likely to put in front of him. He remembered why he had come to the Psychic Circus in the first place. He had been looking on the dark side unnecessarily. This was going to be his big chance to win one of the fabulous prizes the advertising satellite had told him about. He felt almost sorry for that double-crossing Captain who was going to miss out on all the fame and the loot.

When the fanfare sounded to herald his entry into the ring, Nord went in, head held high, the applause of the crowd ringing in his ears. He would show them. This could still be the finest hour of Nord, the Vandal of the Roads.

The others watched him go. The Doctor stopped his juggling when he noticed that Mags was shaking – shaking with an inner terror that he found surprising in one apparently so fearless.

'It scares you, doesn't it, Mags?' he asked gently.

'Oh, he'll be fine,' Mags replied sardonically. 'Just like the other one was.'

'You saw what happened, didn't you?' the Doctor pressed. He knew something had to have occurred before he and Ace had arrived, something in the ring that Mags had seen. He remembered now that Ace had heard screaming as they had approached the Circus, screaming that had abruptly been cut off. Could that have been Mags? 'Are you going to tell me?' he asked softly.

Mags turned away sharply. 'See for yourself,' she said harshly. She was not proud of having seen sights so bizarre and cruel that she had screamed and screamed, she who had never screamed before. Let the Doctor experience them too.

'Don't bother Mags, Doctor,' Captain Cook put in, sipping his umpteenth cup of special blend tea. 'You have to be careful with these rare specimens.'

'What do you mean?'

But the Captain was not to be drawn either. 'You'll see, Doctor,' he drawled enigmatically. 'You'll see.'

Another fanfare rang out. Nord was in the ring now. The canned applause and laughter rose in volume to greet him.

The Doctor moved to the cage door. The clowns had drawn the curtains round the cage but they had left a small gap. Deliberately, the Doctor suspected, knowing the cruelty that operated here. Through it, the Doctor could just see the ring and Nord's broad back as he acknowledged the prefabricated acclaim of the crowd.

Nord, meanwhile, was beginning to enjoy himself. The noise and the lights excited him. Out of the corner of his eye he could see a family of three munching at their crisps as they watched his entrance.

The Ringmaster propelled him into the beam of a spotlight in the centre of the ring. Lying on the floor was a huge barbell. Nord's heart rose. They were going to test his strength. There was nothing to worry about.

He lifted it with ease, indeed with such ease that he held the huge weight above his head with one hand before letting it drop to the floor. The recorded crowd went wild. And the family, who had sat impassively, now all held up score cards. '9' read the father's card. And the little girl's. And the mother's. He was a success, there was no doubt about that. A smirk started to creep across his brutal face.

The Ringmaster held up his hand to silence the canned applause. Nord thought he might be about to receive his prize. But the Ringmaster apparently had other ideas.

'A man of might is Nord,' he cried, 'now he'll go for broke
By making you laugh with a favourite joke.'

Nord was horrified. A joke? He didn't know any jokes. He never told jokes, and the only people who'd ever told jokes to the Vandal of the Roads had had their ears pulled off horribly. Give him some more weights to lift, or a spot of lion-taming, perhaps. But telling a joke! It simply wasn't fair.

It very quickly dawned on him, however, that there was no alternative. He had to tell a joke if he wanted to survive. He cleared his throat nervously.

'A funny thing happened to me on the way to the, er, on the way to, er, the er . . .'

But he knew he was already lost. The family were raising their score cards. They read '0'. And '0'. And '0'.

Nord's screams of protests lasted only a few seconds before they were cut off. Mags, despite herself, had joined the Doctor at the gap through the curtain.

'Was this what you saw before?' the Doctor demanded sternly.

'Not exactly' was the bleak reply. 'But just as bad.'

There was a harsh ear-splitting noise and a brilliant coloured flash of light from the centre of the ring. The Doctor was thankful they could not see more clearly what had happened. When the smoke had cleared, the Ringmaster picked something from the ring floor. It was a tiny charred fragment of the leopard skin. He displayed it triumphantly and the canned laughter burst out again eerily. There were no other visible remains of the mighty Nord, Vandal of the Roads.

'Could you let something like that happen to you?' the Doctor demanded of Mags as the two of them watched wide-eyed. Mags shook her head. As the Doctor had suspected, she would fight for her life. Now, if they could only hit on some means of escape.

His eyes dropped involuntarily to the Indian clubs he had been given to practise juggling with. Mags' eyes dropped to them too. There was something animal-like in Mags' smile when she saw them. The Doctor found himself grinning too. Maybe they had simultaneously had the same idea. Maybe there was a way out of their prison.

'It must be awfully exciting working for the Psychic Circus, Morgana.' The Whizzkid was in full flood, pacing the vestibule and commenting on the treasure trove of Psychic Circus memorabilia that was there. It seemed to the deeply bored Morgana that he had been talking non-stop for hours.

'It must have been particularly exciting when you did your tour of the Boriatic Wastes, of course,' he droned on. 'I think most of your admirers would agree with me that that was one of your finest ever gigs. Well, in so far as you can tell from the posters, of course . . .'

'Wouldn't you like to be getting along inside?' Morgana suggested finally in desperation.

'You mean, I can go in? Just like that?' The Whizzkid was thrilled.

'Yeah. Go in right now. Please.'

'Oh wow!' The Whizzkid lifted up the flap and rushed down the corridor into the Big Top. Where, no doubt, in good time, the Ringmaster would pick him out of the audience and invite him to take his place as a performer. Usually Morgana felt a real twinge of anguish these days when she let people go so eagerly to their fate. If she dared, she even tried to dissuade them, but not, for some odd reason, in this particular case.

7

The Well

'Mags . . .'

'What?'

Captain Cook had been watching their preparations with unruffled indifference. The Doctor sensed Mags' growing irritation with the Captain's defeatist attitude. 'It's not going to work,' the Captain insisted, sipping his tea. 'I remember when I was in the Baleful Plains of Grolon, I . . .'

'I don't care!' The vehemence of Mags' retort pleased the Doctor as much as it surprised him. The Captain, however, merely shrugged philosophically.

'Are you ready?' the Doctor enquired. Mags nodded. They stood by the cage door, Indian clubs in hand, and started to argue about who was going next into the ring. Each claimed the honour and, though the whole thing was prearranged, both of them gave very creditable impressions of angry performers clamouring to get into the ring. It certainly seemed to impress the robotic clowns on guard. If they could keep up their quarrel just a little longer . . .

The two robotic clowns eventually decided that they had to do something about this unseemly uproar. Orders, after all, were orders. They raised the door and entered the cage, which is exactly what Mags and the Doctor hoped they would do. Indian clubs became handy weapons and, before they could do anything about it, the two robot clowns were stretched on the cage floor with their robotic brains temporarily immobilized by two sharp knocks on the head. And the door lay open.

'Are you coming, Captain?' the Doctor asked as he moved towards the way out.

'No, thanks, old man,' Captain Cook replied lazily. 'I'll sit this one out.' The Doctor was surprised but he did not have any time to argue – or to be as suspicious of the Captain's reasons as perhaps he should have been.

Mags, however, took it much harder. This, after all, was her mentor and guide and it was painful to acknowledge their ways were parting. 'Goodbye, Mags,' he said calmly. 'Goodbye, Captain,' she replied with a dismay that was all too obvious to the Doctor. But they could not linger to argue. Someone else would come backstage and discover what had happened soon enough. They had to get far away from the cage as fast as they could.

Ace let herself out of Bellboy's former prison cautiously and looked round: the coast was clear. She chose her way at random; there was no other course she could take. In this maze of corridors it was hopeless to believe she could retrace her steps with any certainty.

She had no idea how long she wandered. Her feet ached and each corridor looked very much like the last. And then coming down one of the indistinguishable, shadow-filled tunnels, she saw in the distance a brightly painted caravan lodged incongruously in the corner. It was beautifully decorated and, by the standards of the rest of the circus, well preserved. It reminded her of gypsy caravans back home. What it was doing there, however, was a mystery.

The door of the caravan opened. Ace fell back against the canvas wall and watched. Two clowns emerged carrying a stretcher, on it a covered body. Ace crept nearer. The next to emerge was the Chief Clown. She heard him say something about taking the thing on the stretcher to be tested now it had been repaired, but she was still too far away to make out all that was being said.

In time she might have been able to puzzle out what was going on, but she had been too intent on watching the

75

scene. She heard a noise behind her, and turned to see a vacant grinning face looking up at her. The man carried a broom and apparently considered it a great joke to play games with her. She tried to get past him, away from the caravan, away from the Chief Clown, but he played an 'after you, no, after you' game it was impossible to escape from.

Ace became angrier by the moment. She could see the man was harmless but this really wasn't a time for games.

Indeed it wasn't. She felt a strong hand on her shoulder. The Chief Clown stood behind her, holding her in a vice-like grip. The red gash of a mouth spread into an ugly smile. 'That'll do, Deadbeat,' he commanded and the other man fell back. Two robotic clowns came up and, at the Chief Clown's command, seized her. 'Let me entertain you,' he purred as they dragged her along. But Ace did not really believe for a moment that what the Chief Clown meant by entertainment was what anybody else meant by it. And she had been doing so well!

'Calling the Doctor! Calling the Doctor! There's no escape. Repeat. There's no escape!'

The Ringmaster's voice followed them wherever they ran. There was no doubt that their escape had been discovered. Their only hope was that nobody had any idea which direction they had taken. However, the repetition of the announcement made the Doctor cross. 'I do wish they would stop saying that,' he grumbled. 'I heard the first time.'

They had been running without any plan, hoping to find a way out to the open air, but now it seemed they had entered a very different part of the circus. Older, darker, more mysterious. Then Mags pointed excitedly ahead of them.

There was an arch there, an old stone arch, incongruous in a way after the flimsiness of the tent walls. Beyond it loomed dark corridors of stone. They had entered a new world all of a sudden, or, more accurately, an old world. For the arch with its ancient hieroglyphic decorations seemed to belong to an earlier and more mystic age.

The Doctor examined the inscriptions on the arch more closely. 'Extraordinary,' he murmured. 'These are the same kind of stones that stand in the Big Top itself.' He furrowed his brow. 'Where can they come from?'

Mags gave him a strange look. 'Maybe they were always here.'

'That thought,' returned the Doctor gravely, 'had also occurred to me.' But then he noticed a change come over Mags. A haunted look came into her eyes and her body tensed as she pointed up to a sign cut into the top of the arch. 'Do you see it?'

'See what?'

'That moon sign.' She could barely get the words out. Now the Doctor saw what she had seen. Cut into the stone and inlaid with silver was a crescent moon, and, next to it, emerging from the clouds, a full moon.

The Doctor was immediately alert and concerned. 'Why does that worry you? Tell me.'

But Mags either could or would not. 'We should get on, Doctor,' she insisted, forcing her eyes away from the moon symbols. And, indeed, over the loudspeakers came the Ringmaster's voice once more.

'Calling the Doctor. There's no escape.'

The Doctor passed under the arch and somehow Mags found the nerve to follow him. 'Will those people never take "no" for an answer?' the Doctor grumbled.

'No,' Mags answered quietly.

They were going down a gloomy stone tunnel now. The walls dripped with water and they could feel the cold, damp air blowing against their bodies. Now and then they caught sight of another weird hieroglyph carved into the stone, but neither of them could pretend to understand where they were going, or why this antique structure was here.

77

Then Mags gave a cry. She had been taking another step forward into the gloom when she realized just too late that the ground fell away without warning. She would have plunged headfirst into the hole that gaped there if the Doctor had not grabbed her in time and pulled her back.

They stopped and stared down into the abyss that confronted them. The hole was pitch dark and apparently bottomless. They could certainly see no end to it.

'Nasty little booby trap that,' the Doctor mused. 'If it is a booby trap, that is. The Pharaohs used something rather similar. I told Rameses the Second they were more trouble than they were worth.' He sighed. 'Still, whatever it is, there's certainly no way ahead now.'

'Is it a well?' Mags asked, gazing down.

'Only one way to find out.'

The Doctor was still carrying his Indian club. Now he found another use for it besides braining robotic clowns. He lifted it and dropped it down into the black hole.

They strained for any sound, a splash or a crash, but none came. They peered down into the gloom. Then slowly, mysteriously, a red-rimmed eye materialized in the depths of the well, unblinking but penetrating. Mags backed away in shock, but the Doctor continued to stare down, taking its measure.

'That eye,' he mused thoughtfully. 'I've seen it before. It was all over the kites in the entrance hall. Fascinating.' He peered into the darkness as far as he could. The eye was still there, not blinking or moving, just watching and waiting. Somehow, somewhere, down there, the Doctor realized with growing excitement, there must be a clue to all that is going on in the Psychic Circus.

A throat was politely cleared behind them. They turned to face Captain Cook, accompanied by a posse of clowns. How foolish, the Doctor thought with a pang, to believe that the Captain would not betray them to save himself.

The Captain coughed once again, apologetically, to make sure he had their full attention. 'Awfully sorry to butt in like this, old chap,' he began. 'But I'm afraid you're wanted, Doctor. You're the next one due on in the ring.'

Mags confronted her old master angrily. 'Why have you brought those clowns here?'

'Survival of the fittest, old girl,' he answered smoothly, adding with just a touch of malice, 'don't tell me you never came across that on the planet Vulpana.'

The Doctor was angry in a different way. He cared less for the betrayal than for his interrupted investigations. 'Captain,' he protested, 'we could be on the point of getting to the bottom of the mystery of the Psychic Circus. Doesn't that mean anything to you?'

'Frankly, old man, no,' the Captain drawled in reply. 'Anyway, what's going on seems pretty clear to me. Anybody dumb enough to get into the ring gets killed.' He gestured back the way they'd come. 'Shall we be going?'

The clowns advanced and the Doctor and Mags realized escape was hopeless. Ahead was the abyss of the well, the only alternative to being hauled back to the ring and probable destruction. The Doctor allowed himself to be led away, as did Mags, but the Doctor could sense a tremendous anger burning within her.

The eye, for all they knew, still gazed balefully from the well. That eye whose shape was reproduced on every kite in the Circus. And whose form, had they known it, appeared often now in Morgana's crystal ball.

'Let me go. Let me go, pastry face.' Ace protested as fiercely as she could. But she had no real chance against the combined force of the Chief Clown and his metallic minions. Step by step, she was dragged towards the mysterious caravan. Before it had looked picturesque. Now the nearer she came to it, the more sinister it seemed. The Chief Clown pulled its door open gloatingly.

'Half an hour in there,' he hissed, 'and you'll tell me what I want to know.' The red gash of a smile slit his white mask of a face. 'Don't like clowns, do you?'

The next moment Ace was inside and the door was shut behind her. The caravan was gloomy and silent. She could see and hear nothing. Then there was a rustling sound in the distant recesses of the caravan. Ace braced herself. Whatever it was was not going to frighten her. She promised herself that.

'Who's there?' she challenged, trying to keep the tremor out of her voice. 'Come on, you don't scare me.'

Whatever lay in the shadows started to move slowly but inexorably towards her.

The Captain led his captives back along the stone tunnel they had discovered so recently. The clowns brought up the rear. The Doctor could still feel Mags' fury and the force of it was frightening in its intensity.

They passed back under the stone arch. And as they did so, Mags glanced up at the moon symbols. To the Doctor's surprise, the full moon began to glow silver, as if it were emerging finally in its entirety from behind the covering clouds.

The Captain noticed too, and it plainly alarmed him. A change was coming over Mags. A change that it would be difficult to describe, except by saying that she seemed more fundamentally animal than ever before. She suddenly changed her stance and turned on the Captain with a threatening physical aggressiveness that caused him and the clowns to fall back. Whatever was happening, it alarmed Captain Cook as nothing seemed to have done since the Doctor had known him.

'Mags,' he pleaded. 'Not now, please not now. Not yet.'

Mags moved forward and the others fell back before her. She turned momentarily towards the Doctor. Their eyes met, and though hers were red-streaked and ferocious now, the Doctor understood their message. He was being offered a chance of escape. The clowns moved to stop him but the snarling Mags kept them at bay.

There would be time later to understand what had

happened in these few puzzling moments. For now the Doctor had to concentrate on making a break for freedom. He took the opportunity gratefully, and ran as fast as he could away from the stone arch and its tableau of confrontation.

He who learns to run away lives to fight another day.

The figures loomed out of the shadows. There were two of them, and Ace could finally make out what they were – robotic clowns, but half-finished, or half-repaired, which gave them an especially alarming appearance. Partly stripped of their bright costumes, cold metallic torsos laid bare, wires hanging loose, heads half finished, they came closer. And though they were incomplete Ace realized that they were quite able to harm her. Which seemed, from their inexorable advance, to be their intention.

Ace reached around for something to defend herself with. A dismembered robot arm lay on some sort of workbench, well within her reach. She could probably do some damage with that, if the worst came to the worst. But as she grasped the disembodied limb, it gave an involuntary movement and grabbed back at her. Ace cried out in surprise and let it drop.

Slowly she was being edged back against the locked door. There were more robot clowns now, she could see, in various states of disrepair. She even began to wish they had their white clown faces fitted on. That would somehow make them easier to handle.

The leading robot stretched out an arm towards Ace. She grabbed it defensively and tugged at it. It came off in her hand quite easily, and now she felt better. She had a weapon to bash the approaching robots with.

'Just 'cos I said I don't like clowns doesn't mean I'm scared of clowns, OK?' she cried as fiercely as she could. 'Got that, tin-can heads?'

The clowns kept on coming, however, pinning her

moment by moment further against the door. 'I said, got that, tin-can heads?'

The leading clown opened its mouth to reply, but only a weird metallic buzzing emerged. The others joined in the babble. The noise became deafening, and Ace, forgetting any plans of attack, put her hands to her ears to keep out the hideous babble.

The buzzing ceased as abruptly as it had begun. The clowns all froze in whatever metallic posture they were in at that moment: heads half turned, legs raised to kick, arms stretched to grab. Ace gave the leading clown a tentative push. It fell over with a clatter. Amazed, Ace dropped the robot arm and looked beyond the clowns.

She could now just make out that she was in a workshop, its floor cluttered with half-finished robots and, now and then, a vast brightly painted carnival head. In one corner sat the dishevelled Bellboy, in much the same bad shape as when she had last seen him, except that now he was tearful and apologetic. In his hand he held some sort of remote control box.

'They shouldn't have . . . I'm sorry,' he murmured distractedly across the gloom to Ace. 'I'm sorry . . . I fell asleep.'

But there was no flicker of recognition in his blank eyes as Ace moved across the cluttered workshop towards him, picking her way through the immobilized clowns.

She knelt beside him. 'We've met before,' she insisted gently. 'Don't you remember me?'

Bellboy simply stared at her. He was beyond all help, Ace thought. But then his eyes suddenly caught sight of the earring she had found by the bus, and a glimmer of understanding entered his eyes at last.

'Flowerchild!' he whispered.

8

The End of Bellboy's Dream

The family sat impassively in the empty Big Top. Bright
circus music came over the loudspeakers but nothing was
happening in the ring. The mother passed round fresh bags
of crisps, but there was a growing air of dissatisfaction.

'I don't think much of this, father,' the mother remarked
in her polite, even tones.

Her husband's eyes surveyed the emptiness. 'Nothing's
happening, is it?'

'Not that I can see.'

'Mummy, mummy . . .' The little girl's whining voice
spoke now.

'What is it?'

'I'm bored, mummy.'

'There's no point in going on, dear,' the father chided
with a touch of sternness. 'We're all bored.' He paused and
there was more than a touch of menace as he remarked,
'Something's going to have to happen soon.'

Morgana was in a state of panic and confusion. The eye
appeared in her crystal ball all too often now, and she could
feel its power reaching out towards her. It was a long time
since they had felt its power with such force and immediacy.
She knew that unless they acted soon the whole fragile
structure of the Psychic Circus would crumble to dust.
Nervous at the lack of activity in the Big Top she rushed
backstage.

The Ringmaster stood coolly by the open cage door.

Morgana's words came out in a rush. 'What's been

happening? Has the Doctor escaped too? The Doctor and the girl, I liked them – but he's trouble for us, I can see it out there.'

'Hey, hey, stay cool, Morgana,' the Ringmaster advised her calmly. 'Don't take your crystal ball act too seriously. They'll be back.'

The Chief Clown also entered the backstage area to hear this, having taken care of Ace. 'Are you sure the other two will be recaptured?' he demanded.

'Yep,' the Ringmaster nodded with a grin 'The Captain's a dead man if anything goes wrong.'

'You let him out to get the others back?'

The Ringmaster nodded. 'Trust me.' But the other two were not so easily reassured.

'You do realize there's no act in the ring, don't you?' demanded Morgana.

'And you know what happens if we don't get an act out there very soon?' the Chief Clown added, still more forcefully.

'Easy, easy.' the Ringmaster grinned. 'If the worst comes to the worst, there's always him.' With that he gestured towards the corner of the cage where the enraptured Whizzkid sat watching the proceedings. The nod in his direction was enough to bring him over, all wide-eyed excitement.

'Hallo,' he said breathlessly, offering his hand. 'You're the Chief Clown, aren't you? I knew you immediately. You see, I've got pictures of all of you going right back to the very early days. In fact, I've got a poster from your very first show on the planet Othrys.'

The Chief Clown for once was lost for words. He could only stare at this deluded imbecile who was now reaching for an autograph book in his back pocket and thrusting it under the Chief Clown's nose.

'Could you sign your name in this, please,' he asked politely. 'You too, please, Morgana.'

Morgana was the only one of the trio who felt even a

twinge of pity as they signed cheery messages of congratulation for their next victim.

'How could you do this to me, Mags?' the Captain enquired reproachfully as they were marched down a circus corridor under guard back to the waiting cage. Mags was her normal self again, all the aggression that had so terrified him gone from her, but her resentment against him had not gone with it. 'After all I've done for,' the Captain moaned. 'The Doctor gets away and you and I are going back under guard.'

'You were lucky,' Mags replied tersely.

The Captain nodded. 'Well, in a way, I suppose. I am still in one piece. You could have given us the full works. But, as usual, in the end, the old team of Mags and the Captain stuck together.' A reminiscence came to him and the memory instantly cheered him. 'As a matter of fact it reminds me of the time on Fagiros when the Architrave of Batgeld was showing me his collection of early Ganglion pottery . . .'

But it was doubtful if either the robot clowns or Mags were paying much attention.

Bellboy held the earring in his hand and studied it sadly. He did not speak, and it made Ace uncomfortable. She never felt at ease when other people were all bottled up and choked with emotion like this. She had picked up one of Bellboy's control devices and was looking it over, knowing that it was right to wait for Bellboy speak first. You couldn't rush people in this state.

'Flowerchild,' Bellboy sighed, eventually, 'They murdered you . . . With a robot I made . . .'

'You're sure that's what happened?' It fitted the facts that Ace had been able to assemble but she had to be sure.

Bellboy gazed at the earring. 'There can be no doubt. Every robot, every clown in the circus I made and maintained.' He gulped. 'For this.' His wasted eyes met Ace's. 'They wouldn't even let me die now. They still need me.'

'You mean, no one else knows how?' Ace gasped.

Bellboy nodded. 'We each agreed to learn one circus skill and become pre-eminent in that.' He gestured round the workshop. 'Mine was this.'

'This control unit is brill,' Ace remarked. She knew it was not an adequate response but she felt out of her depth here.

'Have it,' Bellboy urged impulsively. 'It's no use to me here. It controls that robot over there. And the full scale version I made of it.' He pointed over to a table where a scale model stood. Ace recognized its contours immediately. In miniature it was the robot that Mags and Captain Cook had been excavating what seemed like weeks ago. Was everything then on this benighted planet linked up somehow?

Instinctively Ace's hand went to one of the control buttons to try out her new gift, but Bellboy laid a warning hand on hers. 'Careful. That activates the laser beam eyes.' Ace stopped her experiments immediately. But though her diversion had taken Bellboy's mind off his despair for a few moments, he gazed now at the model and the bitterness flooded back in, triggered by the sight of it.

'It was to have been my masterpiece,' he sighed. 'But, like everything else, it was misused and went wrong.' He paused, feeling painfully for the words he needed, fighting against the cruel punishment he had received in the ring. 'We had such high ideals when we started. We shared everything. We enjoyed developing our circus skills and making people happy. If there were any problems, we'd sit around and talk them out. We were all happy. At least,' his voice trailed away, 'it seemed we were . . .'

'Until you came here – to this place?' Ace tried to keep calm, not show the excitement she felt.

'Yes. And even then at first we thought . . .'

'What?'

'We thought . . . We thought . . .' Bellboy was becoming tired and muddled again now. 'It's so difficult to remember

. . . But we knew once why we came here . . . And it was an important place for us . . .' The wasted eyes met Ace's. 'I'm sorry. I can hardly think. You see . . .' And then he saw the earring again and it was too much. 'Oh, Flowerchild,' he sobbed.

Much to his surprise the Doctor was back in the circus vestibule. He was not quite sure how he had found his way back there, but he wasn't going to look a gift horse in the mouth. There was much to be investigated here.

There were, for example, the kites stacked there. All decorated with that distinctive eye symbol, the image of the sinister reality the Doctor had just confronted at the well. And then there was that crystal ball that Morgana had stared so intently into. What did she see there?

Tiptoeing to the counter where it sat, the Doctor studied the ball carefully. For a moment the ball was clouded over. And then it cleared and an image appeared. It was the red-rimmed eye again, watching and waiting unblinkingly as it had done before. The Doctor regarded it gravely. He had not been handling things as well as he should, he knew. And things were obviously beginning to get beyond anyone else's control.

He heard a sound and hid as well as he could behind Morgana's counter. Someone was approaching the crystal ball. It was Deadbeat. Deadbeat stared into the ball and his vacant eyes met the eye within. There was something about the exchange that caused a change in Deadbeat.

His hands went to the locket which hung round his neck, the locket which was the only part of his attire that had remained bright and clean amid his general decay. From his cramped vantage point, the Doctor could see that he tried to raise the medallion, to bring whatever was on it into contact with the all-seeing eye. But the effort was too much. With a moan of despair, he dropped the locket and ran helplessly from the vestibule.

Deadbeat, then, knew something. The Doctor had not

been wrong to sense the presence of some former authority in him. As he hurried out of the vestibule in pursuit, the Doctor noticed one of the old circus posters. 'Great Fun for all the Family!' it proclaimed. Really, the Doctor thought, I don't know how they have the nerve!

The Doctor had to move fast to keep up with Deadbeat's odd, loping walk. He followed him down the billowing corridors that seemed no more familiar and no more easy to negotiate however many times you went along them. After a while, Deadbeat stopped dead and turned grinning inanely. He had clearly known the Doctor was behind him for some time. There was nothing for the Doctor to do but make the best of that.

'Hallo there, Deadbeat,' the Doctor began, advancing with a smile. 'Fancy seeing you here. Small world, eh?' But Deadbeat simply stared as the Doctor continued. 'I've been wanting us to have a chat as a matter of fact. It frightened you to see that eye again, didn't it? It means the powers behind it are on the move.' He was pushing his luck now, he knew, but desperate situations demanded desperate remedies. 'Something happened to you here, didn't it, Deadbeat? I know you can't always have been like this. Did you try to find something out? Were you punished?' But there was still no reply, only a blank stare.

'Can you understand anything I'm saying?' the Doctor enquired plaintively. Though there was no reply, Deadbeat's eyes were not unfriendly now. 'I'll tell you one thing I do know,' the Doctor pressed. 'You're not going to give me away to the others, are you?'

There was a pause. And then Deadbeat grinned and there was more understanding in his face than the Doctor had ever seen before. Then he started to sing, not very tunefully, it was true, but the import of the words was clear.

'Follow . . . follow the track . . . Follow the track, there's no turning back . . . Follow . . . follow . . .'

So the Doctor followed.

* * *

88

The family sat eating choc-ices. They were still waiting for the next act. It had been promised. And it had better be there soon. Or they would start getting rather angry.

Backstage, the foraging party had returned with empty hands. 'I'm afraid the Doctor gave us the slip,' the Captain was explaining as calmly as he could.

Unluckily for him, it was not the Ringmaster or Morgana he had to do the explaining to but the Chief Clown, who reacted with a dangerously quiet 'He did what?'

'He gave us the slip,' the Captain repeated. 'A very similar thing happened to me once in the Bay of Paranoia on Golobus.'

'I don't care what happened on Golobus,' the Chief Clown snapped.

'Your loss, old boy,' the Captain murmured genially, turning to Mags. 'Anyway, it was all her fault, of course.' Mags opened her mouth to protest at the betrayal, the second betrayal, but Captain Cook did not give her time. 'I imagine you'll have to put her in the ring next as some sort of punishment.'

'No,' the Chief Clown returned smoothly.

'Oh. Found someone else then?' The Chief Clown nodded grimly. 'May I enquire who?'

'You.'

It was not perhaps the best moment for the Whizzkid, all wide-eyed enthusiasm, to come up to the dumbfounded Captain. 'Aren't you Captain Cook, the famous inter-galactic explorer?' he began brightly. 'I've got maps at home showing all your journeys and a piece of one of your old shoes I bought in a souvenir shop on . . .'

The Captain turned away angrily. Normally he would have been delighted to be recognized and admired. But, with his demise in the ring imminent, these were not normal circumstances.

Meanwhile, outside in the vestibule, Morgana stared again at the eye. It was there all the time now. She no longer had any strength to resist its will. All pity for the victims of the circus, all desire to escape, were draining from her moment by moment. The Ringmaster, when he found her, had to shake her hard to get her attention. Even then she pointed to the eye.

'Look! It's here now. What we found. What we serve. It'll always be here now. Waiting for us to fail.' The Ringmaster looked away. Whatever was there frightened him. 'Don't pretend you don't see,' Morgana cried.

'We have an empty circus tent in there,' he returned angrily. 'I don't want to talk about anything else.'

Then the Chief Clown came in. In a way his news was good. There was a new act arranged, Captain Cook. But that did not really alleviate the Clown's chilly anger much. 'I'm much more worried about the Doctor escaping,' he brooded. 'He's really dangerous.'

'Let's go find him then,' the Ringmaster suggested, eager to get away from the crystal ball and what it contained.

'I'll go find him,' the Clown insisted. 'You get back in the ring.'

The dictatorial tone angered the Ringmaster. He did not take orders from anyone. There would probably have been a full-scale row if Morgana had not silenced the two men and pointed to the crystal. It was changing colour. Then the glass cleared and in it there appeared an image of the Doctor following Deadbeat down a corridor.

'It's shown him to us,' Morgana exclaimed in awed tones. If the force they served was manifesting its power and knowledge in this new way, it must want the Doctor caught very badly. The Chief Clown must get after him without the least delay.

It was one of the most extraordinary hours Ace had ever spent. She had never been so close to such naked grief before. Bellboy talked a lot about Flowerchild now. 'Kites,' he explained, 'she made beautiful kites. Every colour of the rainbow. All shapes and sizes; animals, birds, ships, trees.

And they destroyed it all. They used them to watch us and trap us and keep us here. And after they'd destroyed them, they destroyed her.'

Ace tried to promise him that he'd be rescued, but it meant nothing. 'Why should I want to get out of here?' he asked simply. 'It's gone, the fun, the freedom, the being what you want to be. All of it. Don't you understand?'

Ace tried to. But Bellboy could not take in her worries about the Doctor and escape. All he thought of was the end of the Circus. 'They've taken all that was bright and good about what we had and buried it where it can never be found again.'

Ace changed tack and got him to explain who 'they' were, the ones he spoke of who had destroyed the dream. 'They're the ones who run the Circus now,' he explained. 'The ones you've met. But there didn't used to be just them . . . There was . . .' His face strained with effort but his thoughts were still fragmentary and confused. He shook his head despairingly. 'It won't come back. The best were all destroyed one by one . . . Flowerchild and Juniper Berry and Peacepipe and . . .' His brow furrowed. 'And Deadbeat. Except, no, he wasn't called Deadbeat then, he was called . . .' The face went blank. 'No, it's gone. But he was our brightest and our best then. I remember that.'

And then he fixed Ace with a look of utter desolation. 'There's nothing I want now. The dream's over.'

The door rattled noisily. Somebody was trying to come in, to take Ace back to the ring no doubt. They might need Bellboy for the repairs but she was just a nuisance. If it was the Chief Clown, though, he was making a bit of a pig's ear of opening the door, Ace thought. She braced herself, nevertheless, for the worst, searching round desperately for a weapon. Bellboy would be no help. He wanted it to be the end.

Finally the door burst open, and Deadbeat entered. Followed, a moment later, by the Doctor. Ace could hardly believe her eyes as he came across the room to greet her warmly.

'Deadbeat, I take it all back,' he exclaimed, delightedly clutching Ace's hand, realizing that he owed this encounter to Deadbeat's guidance.

Deadbeat had stayed by the door, singing to himself. 'Sift the dreams in your mind,' went the song, 'sift the dreams and you'll be amazed by all that you'll find . . .'

The singing drew Bellboy to him. Their eyes met. 'Kingpin,' Bellboy suddenly said, 'that was your name. Kingpin.'

Captain Cook had had second thoughts. He had decided that maybe it made sense to be nice to the Whizzkid. He had made him a cup of his special tea and, ignoring Mags' angry stare, had started to question the Whizzkid about his interest in the Psychic Circus.

'Well, of course, I've never been able to visit it before,' came the earnest reply. 'But I've got all sorts of souvenirs. Copies of all the advertising satellites that have ever been sent out. All the posters. I had a long correspondence with one of the founder members too, soon after it started. Of course, although I never saw the early days, I know it's not as good as it was when it started, but I'm still terribly interested.'

The Captain's intense concentration did not falter even when the Ringmaster called that he was due on in two minutes. Indeed, he turned winningly to the Whizzkid and enquired solicitously, 'No doubt you dream of having the ultimate Psychic Circus experience as soon as possible?'

'Sorry.'

'You ache for the moment when you do your own act within that sawdust covered magic circle?'

'Oh yes, of course' agreed the Whizzkid eagerly. 'I mean, there's no real danger is there?'

The Captain shook his head benignly. 'Only to those without resource or imagination or panache. I am sure you have all those qualities.' The Whizzkid blushed. 'Come, come, don't be so absurdly modest.'

'Don't listen to him.' Mags had come up now, realizing the Captain's game. But she was wasting her breath. This, the Whizzkid insisted, was one of his heroes, Captain Cook, the intergalactic explorer.

'Exactly,' the Captain put in smoothly, freezing Mags out with a stare, 'and shall I tell you what I'm prepared to do for you? As a special favour? I'm prepared to postpone my brief moment of glory in the ring so you may enjoy the unforgettable experience before me.' He moved his head closer to the Whizzkid's and whispered seductively, 'Far beyond the Bouncing Upas Trees of Boromeo or the Singing Squid of Anagonia.'

The Whizzkid listened mesmerized, an inexperienced mouse before a cat that was a master of the chase. 'Are you sure you can bear to let me go first?'

'It is a sacrifice I am prepared to make.' It was perhaps the most honest statement the Captain had ever made. As the Whizzkid sat there entranced, the cage door shot up and the Ringmaster entered with the attendant clowns who prepared contestants for the ring. He could hardly believe the Whizzkid's eagerness to take the Captain's place but the main thing was to get an act into the ring as soon as possible.

As the attendant clowns fussed round the Whizzkid, Mags tried to reach him but it was useless. 'You know, Mags,' the Captain confided, 'I haven't met anybody quite so gullible since . . .' He paused in genuine surprise. 'You know, I don't think I've ever met anyone quite so gullible.'

'At last.' The family sat up expectantly as the tinny fanfares announced the advent of a new act. The clowns circled the ring in preparation. And then the Ringmaster was there, whip in hand.

'Now welcome, folks, and I'm sure you'd like to know,
We've a great new act for our circus show.
Now welcome, please, with all the warmth you can,
The Psychic Circus's greatest fan . . .'

The Whizzkid stood there entranced, the applause and the cheering ringing in his ears. 'This is the most exciting day of my life,' he announced to the waiting world, 'my dreams come true. I am standing in the ring of the Psychic Circus.'

Mags watched despairingly from the cage. 'You sent that kid out to his death,' she hurled at the Captain.

The Captain was sipping tea. 'Nonsense. He may be a great success. I can remember at the Sacred Games at Muscolane . . .'

The crowd noises cut off suddenly. There was a blinding flash of light, an explosion, wreaths of smoke. A piercing scream. Then the scream, too, was cut off, leaving only silence. 'Survival of the fittest, eh, Mags?' the Captain commented. She turned away, too angry to speak.

In the ring the Ringmaster picked up a pair of spectacles from the floor. They were buckled and twisted and the glass of the lenses was cracked and broken, but they were the sole remaining souvenir of the Psychic Circus's Greatest Fan.

'Sift the dreams, sift the dreams . . . When the mind's divided, the body screams . . .'

Deadbeat sat singing quietly to himself while Bellboy talked of the past, more fluently now he was being willed on by both the Doctor and Ace. 'When Deadbeat was Kingpin, he was one the one who persuaded us to come here. I think there was something he wanted. Something he knew about. We all trusted him.' Bellboy smiled wryly. 'We all trusted each other in those days.'

'But something went wrong?'

'Yes,' Bellboy nodded. 'Something went very wrong.' He furrowed his brow, losing his train of thought. 'This place, you see, it does things to you.'

'And so a friendly hippy circus became a trap for killing people?' the Doctor pursued.

Bellboy nodded again, shuddering. 'Even our own kind.

But that was after Kingpin was no longer Kingpin. Something went with him.'

'And the well?' Bellboy was genuinely puzzled by the Doctor's question. Either he knew nothing or the memory had been blasted from his brain. They tried him on an eye staring out from a well, an eye like those on the kites. But he could not remember. Not any more.

There was a gloomy pause. It was broken by Deadbeat who cackled and then began to sing another of his almost tuneless fragments.

'Look, look, look in the well . . . The eye gives you promises . . . Promises of heaven or hell . . .'

'He's off,' Ace remarked. She had known people like him in Perivale. Sad drunks singing crazily to themselves. But the Doctor held up his hand to hush her. He had been listening to the words. The talk of a well, and an eye. Deadbeat knew something. He knew about it, even if Bellboy did not.

'Tell us, Deadbeat,' he urged as he, Ace and Bellboy gathered intently around the dazed figure. 'Tell us what you know. Please.'

The words came slowly and disjointedly. Often they did not make sense. Often they came in fragments of song. But the Doctor, using what he had already learnt, managed to piece some of the story together. 'Poor Deadbeat,' he mused to Ace. 'He thought he could control whatever dark powers dwell here, but they destroyed him instead. Perhaps it's safer being a Ringmaster and just obeying orders.'

He turned again to Deadbeat. 'If we take you to the well, can you show us what you did there when you tried to control the powers?' Deadbeat nodded. The eyes were still vacant but understanding was creeping back, step by painful step, into his long-slumbering brain.

The Doctor turned to Ace. 'Everyone's at risk unless we confront and destroy the powers that are sapping the energy from this place.'

'How do we know it's not a con, Professor?'

'He has led me here to you and Bellboy, Ace. He must have done that for a purpose.'

'Not if your brains are that scrambled.' Ace retorted and then rather wished she hadn't.

The Doctor shook his head and studied Deadbeat's face. 'There's something going on in there, Ace. I saw it when he looked into the crystal ball.'

Ace grinned. 'You're just an ageing hippy at heart, Professor.'

'I suspect there may be something in that,' he acknowledged. 'But we must be going. Are you coming, Bellboy?'

Bellboy shook his head. 'No.' Ace gasped. 'The Chief Clown will come here after you,' he explained. 'I can delay him for a while.' He smiled weakly. 'It would be good to be useful in some way.'

'But Bellboy . . .' Ace wanted to protest, to stop him. Every instinct denied the idea that people deliberately chose the path of death sometimes.

Bellboy looked at her with real affection and shook his head. 'You still don't understand. Everything I loved has gone. What's the point of living on to do work I hate?'

'So be it. Thank you, Bellboy.' The Doctor acknowledged the sacrifice quietly and without fuss. 'And come on, Deadbeat – or should I call you Kingpin? We have work to do.'

Deadbeat rose and began to sing. A more cheerful, and indeed tuneful, song than Ace or the Doctor had heard before. 'The sun comes up,' it began, 'we see it shine . . . The sun's not anyone's . . . Not yours or mine . . .'

Ace turned at the door to say farewell to Bellboy. The Doctor and Deadbeat had already shaken his hand and gone. Bellboy's despair and sense of loss had got through to her, no doubt of that. She was full of feelings she couldn't get out. Choked, really choked.

'Bye now, Bellboy. All the best,' she mumbled. 'Oh, and, er, thanks for this.' She held up the control device Bellboy had given her.

'Goodbye, Ace.'

Bellboy shut the door after they had gone. He heard Deadbeat singing softly. And, unless he was much mistaken, Ace and the Doctor joined in too.

It was some time later when the Chief Clown found Bellboy sitting among his creations. The eye had led the Clown there. It had not told him his prey would already have flown, but Bellboy was unmoved by his questions and his threats.

'I don't know. I don't care any more,' he replied calmly, staring at the Clown with his sad, now expressive eyes. 'It's all gone, destroyed. You know that too. You were a wonderful Clown once. Inventive, funny, outrageous.'

The words must have struck some chord in the Chief Clown because he struck Bellboy brutally across the face. But Bellboy barely acknowledged the blow. 'I'm not helping you any more, you see,' he explained. He reached for the device he used to control the robot clowns, the device he had used to save Ace.

Even before he did anything, the Chief Clown knew what he was intending. And it scared him. 'Don't be a fool, Bellboy,' he hissed.

'They're not my clowns any more,' Bellboy insisted calmly as he stood up and pressed the control device. Every robot in the workshop started up in motion as he did so.

'You've gone crazy.' The Chief Clown sounded almost scared now.

The robots approached Bellboy from all parts of the workshop now. They clustered around him, almost hiding him from the Chief Clown's sight. As Bellboy pressed the appropriate buttons, they turned to face him and raised their powerful metallic hands to strike.

'Don't hold back now,' Bellboy ordered them, his eyes ablaze with insane joy now at the prospect of release. 'Deal with me as you dealt with Flowerchild.'

Before the Chief Clown's panicked gaze, the robotic

clowns pawed and clutched at their creator, pressing in to complete the task. Bellboy had made them well. It took only a few seconds for them to kill him.

But it took time for the Chief Clown to recover. The red gash of a smile took longer than usual to cross the white mask of his face. He was shaken, no doubt of that. But there was work to be done. The show must go on.

9

That Old Devil Moon

Morgana stared mesmerized into the crystal ball, transfixed by the red-rimmed eye. It seemed to be gathering strength and clarity with every moment. How had she ever thought she could want to resist its power?

'The acts will keep on coming now,' she promised intently. 'And no one will ever dare go near the bus again. Those who remain are your servants to do with as you wish.'

There was no response from the unblinking eye, but she knew it had understood, and approved.

Backstage, Mags paced the cage like an animal. She was still upset over the Whizzkid's death and furious at the Captain's indifference. It was a slow and painful process learning the truth about someone you had admired and hoped against hope to go on admiring.

'Calm down, Mags,' the Captain requested, irritated by her pacing and misunderstanding its reason. 'There'll be some more contestants along soon. We're doing very well.'

'That poor kid.'

The Captain gave his characteristic philosophical shrug. 'Us or him, Mags.' His eyes narrowed. 'And before you get too high and mighty, don't forget where you'd be without me. Dead with a bullet in you on the planet Vulpana.' He paused significantly. 'A silver bullet.'

'I know that,' Mags retorted, still trying to get her thoughts in shape. 'But you didn't do it for me. You did it for yourself.' She came up to him and stared him full in the face. 'I only wish I knew what you were after.'

But the Captain was not to be drawn. 'All in good time, Mags, all in good time,' he murmured calmly. 'A man who has played whist with the Card Carrying Dervishes of Tyrade, and won, always keeps his cards close to his chest . . .'

Ace and the Doctor propelled Deadbeat as fast as they could along the corridors to the stone arch. There was barely time for the Doctor to tell Ace of the effect the silver moon symbols had had on Mags as they rushed underneath them.

'Takes all sorts,' Ace replied without taking in the Doctor's concern very much. She was concentrating on the flagging Deadbeat, or Kingpin as they now tried to call him to give him strength. 'Cheer up, Kingpin,' she whispered. 'We're nearly there.'

The further they went down the stone corridor towards the chamber itself, the more agitated poor Deadbeat became. He whimpered and tried to run away but Ace quietly urged him on and somehow he kept going. The effort it cost him, however, was painful to see.

Finally they stood a few paces from the well's edge. Deadbeat turned pale but he did not run. The Doctor was gentle but firm, willing him on. 'Show us please, Kingpin, what you did. When you first saw the eye.'

For a moment Ace and the Doctor thought that Deadbeat would be unable to move. He stood transfixed. There was something awesome about knowing that the red-rimmed eye waited down there, unblinking and patient. Very slowly, trembling all over, Deadbeat advanced . . .

He stopped on the very edge of the well. He did not dare to look down, Ace noticed, but with agonizing and time-consuming effort he lifted up the medallion he wore round his neck. The Doctor gave a grunt of satisfaction. Deadbeat was repeating the gesture he had made to the image of the eye in the crystal ball back in the vestibule. And underneath the medallion, on its obverse side, they could now see a small, sparkling mirror that glinted in the half light. The shape of the mirror was somehow familiar.

Deadbeat held the medallion up for no more than a few seconds and then collapsed without a sound, completely drained. Ace ran to him. 'Well done, Kingpin,' she urged, kneeling by him. 'Great stuff.' He was still conscious and in no immediate physical danger but the power he had confronted had once again revealed its strength.

The Doctor peered pensively down into the well. The eye had veiled itself in darkness once more, withholding its secret from him. But the Doctor's suspicions were confirmed. 'He must have used that medallion to summon the power that lurks down there.'

'And then it did this to him?' Ace demanded angrily. The Doctor nodded. 'I wish I had some nitro-nine to lob down there,' she added savagely. Then they both remembered something. The obverse side of Deadbeat's medallion and what they had seen there.

Gently Ace raised the medallion from where it lay on Deadbeat's chest as he slowly came to. They had not been mistaken in the half-light. The mirror on its underside had the shape of an eye.

'Like the eye that seems to plague us everywhere,' the Doctor murmured, thinking back over the kites, the crystal ball. And, of course, the well itself. He examined it more closely. The mirror had an eye shape, there was no doubt of that, but something still wasn't right. 'The eyeball has been removed by someone.'

They both gasped; for suddenly a lot of other things had fallen into place, things that had previously seemed unconnected. They did not even have to explain to each other. Of course: the eyeball had been hidden in the bus guarded by the sinister conductor. And Flowerchild had died trying to get it back.

At that moment, as if gaining strength from their new confidence, Deadbeat sat up and began to sing one of his rambling songs. But this one was a song of hope.

'We shall be free . . . we shall be free . . . we shall be free . . .'

As soon as Deadbeat was strong enough, they started to move. But as they walked back down the stone corridor, Ace realized that the problems were still immense. They were so close to understanding it all, yet still so far.

'We'll have to get hold of that other bit of mirror, Professor,' she announced decisively.

The Doctor nodded. 'My thoughts entirely. You'll have to take Deadbeat with you and get it from the bus. But, please, do be careful.'

Ace stared at him. She could tell that the Doctor was in one of his mysterious moods. He knew something that he wasn't telling her. Indeed, she nourished a suspicion he'd known something he wasn't telling her ever since that advertising satellite had appeared in the TARDIS. 'But what are you going to do, Professor?' she demanded.

'Oh, I'm going back to the ring.'

'Are you off your head?'

The Doctor shook his head calmly. 'No,' he assured her, 'but the Psychic Circus needs acts. We have to keep the powers occupied. Otherwise more innocents will die. Even Nord did not deserve to die the way he did.' He paused, his piercing eyes staring right at Ace. 'If they have me, perhaps they won't worry too much about you for the moment.'

Ace stared at him in sheer disbelief. 'Sometimes I think it's you that's crazy, not Deadbeat here.'

The Doctor seemed to regard that as a compliment. 'Everybody remotely interesting is mad in some way or other,' he replied. 'Besides, after all the aeons and aeons of time travel, I have developed a remarkable survival instinct.'

'You'll need it, Professor.'

He shrugged, and urged her and Deadbeat to be off. The Doctor was never one for long farewells, especially when there was work to be done. Ace obeyed without too much argument. Much remained unclear but the necessity for retrieving the missing eyeball was clear. The Doctor had turned back towards the ring once more, so Ace followed Deadbeat who led her along a route that seemed incredibly rambling and long-winded but eventually brought them to one of the side entrances of the circus more quickly than she would have believed possible.

They crept unobserved out of the tent. In the distance they could hear from the ring the laughter that was so heartening until you knew its real nature. Nord's bike with its distinctive horned handlebars was parked nearby, but a brief examination was enough to tell Ace it would be useless to them. Poor Nord had never got round to fixing that valve properly.

They would have to rely on their own steam to get them across the open country to the hippy bus as fast as they could.

Understandably, Ace assumed that the bus conductor was still inoperative after its encounter with the Doctor. There was, she was sure, nothing to fear on that count. She had not realized the efficiency and speed with which the Chief Clown always organized repairs.

'I don't know where they find these acts, mother, do you?' The father munched determinedly at his crisps.

'Never seem to get any better, do they, father?' she replied, reaching into her own packet.

The little girl said nothing. All three of them seemed to look less and less like a nice, ordinary, everyday family with every moment.

Mags and Captain Cook looked up in amazement. The Doctor had given himself up to a couple of robot clowns in the corridor outside and was walking back into the cage to greet them.

'You will be pleased to know that the greatest act in the galaxy has returned to the fold, Captain,' he announced brightly.

'Jolly good show,' the Captain returned happily. Mags

rushed up to the Doctor, her eyes blazing, 'I helped you to escape, Doctor, and now you . . .'

'I know, Mags,' the Doctor reassured her in an under-tone, 'but I have not wasted the time you bought me.' He raised his voice so that Captain Cook could also hear. 'In fact, I've returned with an idea.' He seated himself calmly by the Captain. 'I would like to suggest that this time we all work together.' He had the attention of the other two although the Captain affected indifference and sipped at his tea.

'Up to now,' the Doctor continued, 'the people in the cage have been played off against each other.' His eyes sought the Captain's. 'And, of course, some people are more clever at preserving themselves than others.'

The Captain shrugged. 'Luck of the draw, old man.'

'Not entirely,' the Doctor commented drily. 'But what I am proposing is that we all go in together. One for all and all for one. That,' he concluded, 'should throw a very big spanner in the works.'

'I'm with you, Doctor,' Mags agreed enthusiastically, almost before the Doctor had finished speaking. 'And so's he.'

'Now wait a moment . . .' Captain Cook was about to protest but Mags turned on him with such fierceness that he quailed before it, and agreed much more easily than the Doctor could ever have expected to the Doctor's proposal. With the Captain one could, of course, never be sure what ulterior motives he might have but in these circumstances the Doctor knew it was a risk he would have to take. If the Captain were not involved, the dangers of betrayal by him were even greater.

The Ringmaster greeted their offer with an ominous eagerness. Novelties of this kind were, it was clear, hard to find these days. It was with remarkable speed that the make-up clowns prepared them, to the Doctor's relief without insisting on dressing them in any special costumes. But it worried him that everything was happening so fast.

He was, after all, trying to keep the powers occupied for as long as he could. He had told Ace he had a remarkable survival instinct. He did. But there was always a first time . . .

The cage door lifted. The make-up clowns drew back. The Doctor advanced, Mags and the Captain just behind him, towards the ring – the ring in which they had seen others die. As they passed through the entrance, they could hear the artificial roar of the crowd rising in volume to greet them and the shouting of the Ringmaster.

'And now let's welcome not one act but three
To the Greatest Show in the Galaxy!'

The Doctor came into the ring. It was strange to realize that for all the sound and light it was, in fact, empty. Empty, that was, except for the constantly munching family, who, the Doctor noted, were looking rather more animated than they had appeared before.

Mags was just behind the Doctor, but Captain Cook held back. The Doctor was disturbed to notice that he was having a quick word with the Ringmaster who nodded in agreement. Mags eyed him suspiciously but, a moment later, the Captain joined them in the centre of the ring with a charming apology for the delay.

Then the applause was capped by loud cheering, loud enough, it almost seemed, to raise the roof of the tent. The oddly assorted trio stood in the ring and acknowledged the acclaim.

The sight was apparently so arresting that the family even stopped eating. Then the noise died down, the Ringmaster left the ring, and the trio were alone.

It was the Captain who stepped forward first. The Doctor had formulated plans, plans designed to buy Ace time, but they were vague, relying, as he so often did, on his extraordinary intuitive and improvisational skills. But he was still glad to see the Captain taking the initiative for presenting the act. The Captain could, after all, talk the hind legs off a robotic donkey.

The Doctor should, of course, have known better. He did know better the moment the Captain began to speak. But by then it was too late.

The Captain held up his hand for silence. The eerie cheering faded to silence. 'Thank you very much, ladies and gentlemen,' he began, 'but before we start, I would like to make one small request of stage management.' He smiled grimly. 'A special lighting effect.'

'No.' Mags spoke softly but her body was already tense with horrified expectation. The Doctor could only stare as the Captain raised his eyes to where the Ringmaster now stood perched among the seating, a spotlight before him.

'Could you perhaps,' the Captain called, with a deadly politeness, 'give us that old devil moon effect?'

The spot hit Mags, isolating her in the rapidly darkening ring. But, the Doctor realized with a sickening shock in his stomach, it was not an ordinary light that came from the spot. It had the distinct silvery hue of moonlight.

The effect on Mags was immediate. She cowered and ducked, trying to escape from the light's beam, but it pursued her wherever she ran. Moment by moment, her will to run was being worn away. She was being drawn more and more under the power of the moonlight.

The Captain backed away into the gloom but the Doctor could hear his voice, still quiet but with a note of savage triumph.

'You really were remarkably stupid this time, Doctor. I told you she was an unusual specimen. The growling; the snarling; the reaction to the moon. Surely you should have guessed.'

Mags was writhing on the floor now, her face contorted and her moans of rebellion lost in fierce animal-like growls. And indeed the Doctor should have guessed. He had suspected, of course. Had his mind been fatally concentrating on the enigma of the circus and ignoring what was before his very eyes?

There could be no doubt now. The moonlight was

106

working its awful transformation. The hands had grown longer and hairier. The nails had turned to claws. The eyes were becoming blood shot and savage, the face darker and more bestial, the hair like fur. And, worst of all, the mouth. Mags was slavering now. Huge teeth sprouted in her gums. Her tongue lolled hungrily. Then she snarled, baring her terrible fangs. This was no longer Mags: this was a werewolf. And if the Captain had his way, the werewolf would kill the Doctor.

The robot head. The bus conductor. Third time unlucky? The Doctor thought anxiously as he backed as far as he could from the transformed Mags. But the Captain had in his hand now a whip, handed him by the Ringmaster, and from his vantage point at the back of the ring he was urging Mags up from the ground and towards the Doctor.

'Well, quite a surprise, folks, I have to agree
But this could be the Greatest Act in the Galaxy!'

At the ringside the Ringmaster grinned in approval as Mags rose and came towards the Doctor, snarling ferociously. There was no humanity in her eyes now, no knowledge that she had ever known or liked the Doctor. He was simply her prey.

As the Doctor edged away round the ring, Captain Cook's voice continued insidiously from the darkness. 'She hates it when this happens, Doctor. But she can't control herself, of course. And, like all her kind, she has to destroy whatever comes in her path.' There was an exultant pause. 'Which I'm rather afraid, old man, in this case has to be you . . .'

Mags made a feint towards the Doctor who leapt back as best he could. Out of the corner of his eye, he could see the family, all strangely alert now, and all holding up cards reading '9'. This was apparently their idea of family fun. But the Doctor could not afford to take his attention off Mags for a moment as she padded round the ring stalking him. In the background the Captain's voice still goaded him.

107

'This Circus is not the half of it, you see, old chap. These hippy fellows weren't quite as dumb as they looked. They didn't come here just for the fun of it. Well, some of them did, but they're all dead.'

An ugly wheeze of a laugh followed, and then a crack of the whip to urge Mags on. The Doctor knew he must keep on concentrating on Mags. But he must also listen to the Captain, for the Captain might tell him something he needed to know.

The ring was silent now apart from the Captain's voice. But it had never felt less empty. Powerful eyes, the six eyes of the family, were trained on the Doctor now.

'We experienced explorers know all about making the most of our discoveries, you see,' the Captain went on. 'There are powers here to be harnessed by those intrepid enough to grab the opportunities. Myself, for instance.'

'Those powers destroyed Deadbeat,' the Doctor cried back across the ring into the shadows.

'Yes,' came the complacent reply. 'But he was like you, Doctor. None too bright in the old self interest stakes. Still, I do have you to thank for finding a lot of this out for me.'

The Doctor tried to move towards the Captain, to upbraid him for his folly, but it was hopeless. Mags immediately intervened, snarling savagely, and the Doctor had to scuttle back out of her reach.

'Don't try to stop me, old man, that werewolf is extremely dangerous.'

The werewolf's jaws gaped open now and it was slavering. Still the Doctor tried to keep on talking. 'You're meddling with things you don't understand, Captain.' His eyes had just spotted something dangling above the ring. A trapeze, the Doctor thought. Could he reach it?

'No, Doctor,' the voice in the darkness returned, 'you are. Once you're out of the way, I shall make my deal with the powers that be, whoever they be. I remember once when visiting the Gold Mines of Katakiki, I . . .'

The Doctor had finally had enough. As he edged nearer

the trapeze, he called out, 'Captain Cook, you are not only a scoundrel and a meddling fool, you are also a crushing bore!'

The reply this time was a fierce crack of the whip. The Doctor had finally touched a raw nerve. 'I'm afraid you've really done it this time, old man,' the Captain hissed. There was another crack of the whip.

Mags leapt at the Doctor without warning. If it had not been for the trapeze she would have torn him limb from limb. But at the last moment the Doctor managed to get his hands on it and swung out of reach, leaving Mags snarling beneath his dangling feet.

The Doctor and the girl had escaped him. Deadbeat was nowhere to be found. Bellboy had killed himself leaving the robots without anyone to repair them. The Chief Clown was in an angry mood when he entered the vestibule, and anger made him colder and more dangerous still.

Over the loudspeakers snarling and roaring noises came from the ring. 'What's happening in there?'

Morgana looked up from her crystal ball, a strangely gleeful look in her eye. 'The Doctor's in the ring.'

'And the girl?'

Morgana beckoned him over and pointed to the crystal ball. It changed colour. An image appeared, an image of Ace and Deadbeat running across the dusty wastes of Segonax. They had just come to the brow of the hill overlooking the site where the hippy bus lay. So Ace was taking Deadbeat to the bus, thought the Chief Clown. He could guess now what they were seeking; and what the outcome would be. He gave his chilling smile. He did not need to chase them. They were already taken care of.

He and Morgana could go in and enjoy the show.

The ring was filled with frantic activity. The Doctor swung this way and that, desperately seeking a haven from Mags' snapping jaws. Mags followed him all over the tent, driven on by the Captain's whip and the implacable moonlight spot wielded by the Ringmaster. It was a sight that gladdened the Chief Clown's cold heart as he and Morgana entered.

The Doctor felt his arms tiring. He would have to come to rest soon or else he would drop exhausted to the floor at the werewolf's mercy. He made one last effort and swung across the ring, heading by chance towards the place where the family sat, all attention, their food abandoned.

He landed right in front of them. Suddenly, unnervingly, the three of them rose to their feet. The Doctor gasped. Their eyes were glowing, glowing in a way that reminded him of something else. He should have known. He should have realized.

In his surprise he had let the trapeze drop from his hands, and now it had swung out of reach. At the same moment he realized, with that slow kind of realization that appears to take minutes but actually takes less than a second, that he was falling backwards. Knocking down the seats in his path, he rolled towards the ring where the werewolf waited for him, jaws gaping.

10

Kingpin

The werewolf came nearer. It was hard to remember that this was Mags. Mags who had helped him, Mags who had shown compassion for those who died in the ring. But the Doctor had to hold on to the knowledge of what Mags had been. It was his only possible way forward now.

'Mags,' he began with a quiet urgency, 'do you hear me?'

There was no recognition in the werewolf's eyes but at the sound of his voice, she had stopped advancing. The Doctor pressed his advantage.

'Mags, the Captain says that when you're like this, it's in your nature. You have to destroy everything that crosses your path. I don't believe that.'

She was definitely listening now, and there was confusion in her eyes. The Doctor started to gain confidence and speak with a growing authority. 'When you are Mags,' he continued, 'you know what is good and what is not, whom you can trust and whom you cannot. I don't believe that you no longer have any control over those things now you're transformed.'

'Turn up that moonlight a bit, will you?'

Captain Cook had emerged from the shadows now, whip in hand, angry at the delay. Grinning, the Ringmaster did as he was asked. The Chief Clown and Morgana leaned forward expectantly. The family stood, their eyes glowing, waiting for the end.

Mags had started forward again, growling ferociously, and the Doctor knew he had very little time unless she had in some way comprehended what he had said.

'I'm at your mercy, Mags,' he said softly. 'But you don't have to kill anyone.' Mags stopped again. Their eyes met. The Doctor held his breath. He could not be sure what she was going to do.

Captain Cook was getting impatient with the delay. He approached Mags, inciting her to pounce.

'Come on, Mags,' he wheedled, 'You can trust me, you know that. Once he's out of the way, we'll split the proceeds.' The werewolf froze, listening to his soft persuasive words. 'Do it for me, Mags. Do it for your old chum, the Captain.' He grinned. 'You know you'll enjoy it . . .'

The werewolf gave a ferocious snarl. The cynical words had struck home but not in the way the Captain had intended. Mags turned decisively from the Doctor to face the Captain instead. She advanced and the Captain turned pale and cracked his whip angrily.

'Mags, do as I tell you. Mags, I order you to . . . Mags . . .'

The Doctor tried to call out and stop her, but he was too late. With a blood-curdling roar, Mags leapt at the Captain. He stepped back, desperately calling for help. In his panic, he tried to clamber up to the seating. This knocked the base of the moonlight spot, which veered wildly all over the place, despite the efforts of the Ringmaster. None of this helped the Captain to evade Mags. She seized him in her jaws and dragged him back down into the ring.

The Doctor watched, horror-struck. He had never wanted this. He had told Mags she did not need to kill anyone. But events, it seemed, were moving out of his control. In the wildly swaying light of the spotlight, he saw the two figures struggling, and heard the Captain scream. A moment later the screaming stopped.

There was nothing but silence now. The Captain's whip lay useless on the floor where he had dropped it in the struggle. The Doctor studied the sight but, before he could do more, he heard a strange voice booming out across the tent. A deep, authoritative male voice.

'Bring on another act. Now!'

It had come, the Doctor realized with a shudder, from the mouth of the little girl. Her eyes were glowing and the light in them was yet more sinister, as was that in the eyes of the parents that flanked her. Things were happening fast now, frighteningly fast. But the Doctor's first instinct was still to help Mags.

She was lying exhausted at the edge of the ring. She was starting to transform back now and, as her own features became visible once more, the Doctor could see how awed and frightened she was. Her whole body shook helplessly with emotion as she uncomprehendingly watched the robotic clowns gather up the Captain's body, cover it with a gaudy cloth and carry it from the ring on a stretcher. It was clearly difficult for her to understand what had happened, to make the connection between the Captain's damaged corpse and herself.

'Mags, come on. We must get away. Now!' The Doctor helped the still dazed Mags to her feet. The little girl's newfound deep voice was booming its demands across the ring but that was for later. Poor Mags had to be got away from this terrifying place.

At the entrance the Chief Clown and Morgana blocked their way, but Mags was still sufficiently her animal self to scare them when she snarled and growled at them, and they fell back to let the pair pass. Anyway, they have other problems on their hands, the Doctor thought grimly. Everyone did, if what he anticipated was indeed happening.

Ace felt elated. Things had gone better than she could have hoped and they seemed to have reached the hippy bus in record time. Deadbeat wouldn't come in, of course. He sat outside, his eyes still vacant, nervously repeating over and over one of his rambling songs.

'Search . . . search . . . search out the truth . . . search it, search it out . . .'

Ace wasn't worried. She'd found her way into the driver's

113

cabin and after a few moments' searching had found an extra pedal among the instruments placed by the driver's feet. Pressing it had produced from a hidden compartment a small metal chest decorated with hippy symbols like those on the bus itself. She didn't need Deadbeat to tell her this was what she was looking for.

'Kingpin, I've got it!' she called as she leaped out of the bus and ran towards where Deadbeat sat, self-absorbed. However, the chest did not yield its secrets quite so easily. She struggled hard to try to open it without any visible success.

'What I'd do for my chemistry set now,' she muttered, pulling still harder on the lock. 'You'll have to give me a hand with this, Kingpin. Kingpin?'

But Kingpin was not looking at her or even staring at the ground. Instead, he was looking somewhere over her left shoulder, a curious expression on his face. 'Oh, come on, Kingpin, do try to concentrate.'

He gestured vaguely behind her. But the warning was too late. Ace suddenly felt with horror a pair of strong metallic hands tighten round her head.

'Tickets please . . .'

The bus conductor! It had been repaired and now it seemed it was some sort of ticket inspector. Ace didn't have time to work out more than that. She was struggling for her life as the conductor tightened its fearsome grip. She tried to elbow her assailant in its metallic stomach but the only result was a painful bruise.

The chest dropped from Ace's hands. In the struggle the conductor's heavy foot trod on it, breaking it open. It was tantalizing to know she was so near grasping what she wanted and yet totally unable to reach it.

'Kingpin . . . Kingpin . . . Come on! . . . Help me! . . .'

But Deadbeat did nothing. He was staring at the contents of the chest, completely transfixed. Ace fumbled in her pocket for the control device Bellboy had given her, but the conductor knocked it swiftly from her hand.

'May I see your ticket, please, miss?' The grip was tightening all the time now, and Ace could feel herself sliding into unconsciousness. In desperation she lashed out with her foot at the conductor's shins, but again she hurt only herself when the two made contact.

If only Deadbeat would do something to help, she silently pleaded, but he still seemed transfixed by the chest. Now he was taking the glowing eyeball that lay within and holding it up wonderingly.

'Kingpin, please . . .'

Only a matter of moments now and it would all be over, however good a fight she'd put up. Now Deadbeat was lifting up his medallion, still in some sort of trance, and placing the eyeball within the eye symbol on its reverse side.

'Kingpin, help!'

The blackness was enfolding her. In the midst of it she heard a voice, Deadbeat's voice. It had a strength and intelligence she had never heard in it before, like that of someone waking from a dream.

'I remember now. It's beneath the cap.'

'What?'

'Knock its cap off.'

Ace struggled against the blackness to obey Deadbeat's instructions. She scrabbled for the robot's head and managed to push the cap off.

'Now what?'

'Bellboy put in a button saying "Request Stop".' Press it.'

'What?' Ace summoned her last ounce of strength.

'Press the button.'

With a last effort she managed to feel for the button and press it. The effect was instantaneous. The robot conductor stopped stock still.

'Now stand back.'

'What?'

115

'Stand back! Quick!!' There was real authority in Dead-beat's voice now, and real urgency. Ace scrambled towards him across the dry, dusty ground as fast as she could, retrieving Bellboy's control device on the way. The robot still did not move, but out of the silence it spoke.

'All change, please!'

It exploded into a thousand pieces. Ace watched with a mixture of relief and delight. 'Now we're getting some-where!' She turned to Deadbeat and for the first time could see a physical change in his face. The vacant eyes sparkled with intelligence. The face was forceful and mobile. The mouth no longer dropped open but wore a determined smile.

'You really are Kingpin again, aren't you?'

Kingpin nodded gratefully, and held up his medallion showing the eye symbol. At its centre the eyeball glowed. Kingpin studied it for a moment. 'But no one is safe until we get this back to the Doctor at the Circus.'

'Another act! Now!' The little girl's terrifyingly deep voice demanded. And the parents echoed her demand in dark, distorted tones.

'We want more!'

'We need more!'

The voices echoed eerily round the ring. The Ringmaster stood in the centre of the ring, pleading with them. All his arrogance had gone now, and all his authority. He was pleading for his life.

'Another act's coming soon, folks, you can believe me.'

Morgana rushed to join him. Only the Chief Clown held back to watch for developments.

'Another act! NOW!' The insistence and the force increased with each demand. Morgana and the Ringmaster were suddenly very scared. They tried to justify themselves, to defend themselves.

'You haven't played fair with us.'

'We've done everything we were supposed to do.'

116

'I had my doubts,' Morgana cried in an agony of apology, 'but I came through in the end. And there'll be other visitors.'

But they knew their audience was implacable. Not one of the three judges had shown mercy to those who had suffered before in the ring. Why should it be shown to them by the Circus's masters now?

'We need more,' the girl's deep voice called, silencing their protests. 'You have no one to give.' She paused. 'Except yourselves.'

The whole circus tent filled with the bright music Morgana and the Ringmaster knew so well. The brightly coloured robot clowns made their traditional entry. This time, though, they had brought with them two brightly painted magic boxes. Morgana and the Ringmaster watched in horror, unable now to offer any resistance as they were unceremoniously bundled into them by the clowns.

The boxes were sealed. The robot clowns made magic passes as the family watched, then pulled open the two boxes. Inside each there was another smaller box; and inside that another box; and inside that another box; and inside that another box.

And inside the last two small boxes there was quite simply nothing at all. Not even a scrap of clothing, or a trickle of dust.

The Chief Clown watched from the shadows, fascinated but unmoved by the end of his old colleagues. Then, calling a group of robot clowns after him, he left the ring. There was still work for him to do.

The Doctor and Mags had found their way back to the vestibule. Mags was almost back to normal now, though her face showed what she had been through. Morgana's crystal ball was glowing ominously on its counter. The Doctor could not resist stopping to examine in it, despite Mags' anxiousness for them to get on.

117

'Something's happening, Mags. Look!'

Indeed the glass of the crystal ball almost seemed to be pulsing in and out, so violent was the energy bottled within. Mags tried to pull the Doctor away but he was too preoccupied by what he saw. The increasing devastation in the ring was all too plainly reflected in the crystal sphere.

'I may have to go back to the ring,' he announced gravely. 'Things are getting out of control quicker than I thought.' He peered at the image of the family. 'They have destroyed their own servants and still they want more. They wouldn't show themselves to me in here otherwise.'

He was too absorbed to notice Mags' puzzlement and anxiety. A wind was blowing up, rustling the posters and kites that lay around the vestibule's walls, a harsh wind that was gathering force by the moment. Then the father's growling voice came over the loudspeakers.

'Calling the Doctor to the ring! Calling the Doctor to the ring!'

Under the father's voice they could hear a fearsome babble of sound, distorted and threatening. All pretence of happy laughter had gone now. The Doctor listened carefully, the wind starting to howl around him. He turned decisively to Mags. 'Nothing, it appears, will satisfy them now but my presence. Not quite the sort of performance I originally had in mind. Not even the sort of performance *we* had imagined, but there you are.'

'I'm coming back in there with you,' Mags insisted.

The Doctor shook his head firmly. 'No, you must run and fetch Ace and Deadbeat as fast as you can.' He nodded towards the ring. 'I'll do my best to keep them entertained until you all get back with the medallion.' Mags started to protest but he cut her short. 'The Chief Clown won't stay in there to die with the others. He'll be after the medallion too. It's his only hope now.'

Mags still hesitated but, as if to confirm the Doctor's words, the wind lifted the flap at the entrance to the ring and she saw, at the far end of the canvas corridor, the Chief

Clown followed by his robotic minions. 'Go – please!' the Doctor urged, and Mags finally turned and ran as she was bidden.

The Chief Clown stalked past the Doctor without a second look, the final confirmation of how matters had changed. The Clown knew he had no hope of doing a deal with the forces within the ring simply by offering fresh victims. He had to have a bargaining tool. There was only one treasure whose potency and value the family would acknowledge: the medallion that Deadbeat carried, now in its complete form. He guessed Mags' mission in a moment.

Mags had only a short lead but she was swift-footed and her animal-like constitution stood her in good stead. By the time the Chief Clown and his cohorts had reached the entrance, she was already streaking away across the dusty plains.

The Chief Clown watched her go but his ugly gash of a smile did not fade. She had gained a few seconds but what did that matter? He had the hearse. The clowns would run her to ground in no time at all. He gestured to the robots to take their seats, and the hearse quickly started up. It slid off in its silent pursuit of a prey it must surely overtake in a very few minutes.

In the vestibule, meanwhile, the Doctor stood for a moment, gathering his strength and concentration. Around him, the wind was whirling still more fiercely, lashing the billowing canvas walls of the tent and ripping the posters and leaflets off them, sending them fluttering over the floor. The lights, too, had started to pulse with a dark, intermittent, ominous intensity. A storm was gathering.

The Doctor advanced once more towards the flap that lead to the tent. Again the wind lifted it. The corridor was no longer there. All that was visible was a blinding confusion of lurid coloured lights and half-seen shadows. The Doctor knew that he was not being called back into the ring at all. He was being called elsewhere. He had always had a shrewd idea of what he would have finally to confront, but that did not, of course, make it easy to go and confront it.

The wind whistled fiercely. The Doctor held up the flap, and hesitated. However many times he had succeeded, there was always the chance of failure. And these most certainly were not the ideal circumstances in which to give an impressive performance. Those waiting would look for every weakness and he could not afford to show any. He took a deep breath and crossed over into the shadows.

11

The Gods of Ragnarok

The stallholder was not in a good mood as she headed for home. She was very rarely in a good mood, but that did not decrease her sense of being hard done by on this occasion. Not one piece of her delicious fresh fruit and vegetables had been sold since that nice young man on the bicycle had turned out to be another lout on his way to the Psychic Circus. There had been not a single customer since then. She was not perhaps very logical in her ill temper, as the only people who went past her stall were people on their way to the Psychic Circus. If no one went to the Psychic Circus, it might clear Segonax of riff-raff but it would also put her out of business. However, unprejudiced rationality was not her strong point.

She led her horse and cart around a corner. Rushing towards her was a wild-looking young girl, who leapt between the horse and the cart and disappeared down the track. The stallholder watched her go in indignation. Bad manners and way-out clothes! A real hippy weirdo if ever she'd seen one!

Worse was to come. She had barely turned back to take hold of her horse, when a large black limousine careered round the corner. It moved so quietly that she did not hear it coming. Before she knew where she was, it had swerved to avoid her, failed, and become entangled with the back end of the cart. The tail-flap received a tremendous knock, dropped down with a crash and, before the stallholder's horrified eyes, her delicious fruit and veg started to pour out on to the road.

'Circus riff-raff' she cried out angrily as the occupants got out of the car and started to try to disentangle it from the cart and its contents. 'You don't own this planet, you know.'

But the Chief Clown was not listening. As the robotic clowns cleared the way forward, he was calculating how much time this delay would gain Mags. Not, he concluded, enough.

'You know what I really like about you, Kingpin?'

'No, what?'

'You've stopped singing.' Ace and Kingpin were making good progress along the track to the circus. Their spirits were high after their escape from the bus conductor and Ace had started to convince herself that this battle with the forces of evil was all over bar the shouting.

It was when they spotted Mags running towards them that Ace realized she might be jumping the gun. As Mags came up to them gasping for breath, Ace could see the anxiety in her face.

'Where's the Doctor?' Ace asked anxiously.

'Back at the Circus,' Mags panted.

'So you're on your own?' Ace persisted, wondering what fresh plan the Doctor had concocted since they had last spoken.

But Mags had no time to spare for explanations. She pointed behind her. 'I'm not exactly on my own,' she commented sardonically. 'Look.'

Further back down the road Ace saw the hearse speeding towards them, containing, no doubt, the one person who really terrified her on this benighted planet: the Chief Clown.

Mags eyed the medallion that now lay gleaming on Kingpin's chest. 'That's what he's after,' she announced.

Kingpin nodded gravely and sighed. 'I might have guessed.'

'So how do we get it to the Doctor?' There was a sudden

silence that seemed to last an age. The question was a simple one, but the answer, alas, was far from clear. All the time the Chief Clown's hearse was approaching. In a couple of minutes it would be upon them and that would be the end, not only for them but for the Doctor as well.

'Dumbo!' Ace cried with such force that the other two stared at her in startled surprise. 'No, not you two,' she apologized. 'Me.' How could she have forgotten the control device that Bellboy had given her? It hadn't helped her defeat the robot conductor, but that was not what it was designed for. It was designed to control something else, and it was worth a try.

She started to run up the track the way she and Kingpin had come. 'Come on,' she beckoned to the others. They started to run without understanding why.

'But we're going the wrong way,' Mags insisted.

Ace even managed a grin as they sprinted down the track away from the approaching hearse. 'No,' she reassured the others conspiratorially. 'Not for this.' It was the only explanation she had time to offer.

The Doctor felt around him in the darkness. It felt like he was on a stone floor. Perhaps it was a stone floor. The couple of minutes since he had passed under the flap that lead to the ring had been bewildering, even for a Time Lord. Time and space and matter had all seemed dissolved, blown around by unseen winds and reassembled in disturbing new patterns. Somebody less well equipped for such experiences might well have felt their whole sense of self dissolve under the bombardment of sound and light and colour, never to recover again. Even the Doctor felt a little shaky.

It was a stone floor. He could see it now as he lifted himself up and turned his eyes to take in his surroundings. He was standing in an immense stone chamber built from massive blocks, each covered in hieroglyphics. The hieroglyphics were similar to those he had first seen on the corner stones in the ring. Indeed, they reinforced his impression that in shape and construction this was still the circus ring, yet not the circus ring.

The Doctor had been right about where he had been summoned. He stood up, brushed down his hat, his coat and his umbrella and faced the figures he had expected to find there with a confident smile on his face, all doubts apparently put behind him.

'And here you all are at last,' he called out, his voice echoing across the vault-like chamber to his silent listeners. 'I'm not surprised you've brought me here. You must have been finding it very difficult up to now existing concurrently in two different time phases.' He beamed knowingly, willing himself to be unintimidated. 'I know the problem myself . . .'

His audience still did not answer. There were three figures, of course, father, mother and daughter, and they sat on their stone thrones very much as the family had sat on its wooden ones in the circus tent. But these were no longer people. They were deities. Dark, savage deities, wearing heavy stone-like robes, with faces that were set like stone too, but emanating a cruelty and malice never found in simple stone. In the centre of their mask-like faces sat the red-rimmed eye symbol that had pursued the Doctor ever since he had arrived on Segonax. No wonder, he thought, that those battered pillars had seemed so familiar when first he had seen them and had had some inkling of what was going on here.

He raised his hat to the deities in mock deference. 'The Gods of Ragnarok, I presume.'

And then, and only then, did the deities indicate in any way that they had sensed his presence. No greeting. No word. Just a focusing of their cold, stone eyes upon his figure, dwarfed by its surroundings. But not, the Doctor reminded himself, overawed by them. If the Gods of Ragnarok would not speak, he must continue, tearing the

124

mystery away from them and showing that he understood their purposes.

'In ancient times,' he began, 'you would have sat and watched gladiators killing each other here in this ring for your entertainment. If they pleased you, they might live on a little. If not, they died.' A note of contempt entered his voice. 'You were fed either way.'

The silent figures did not reply. The Doctor advanced to the centre of the chamber, warming to his theme.

'And since those times, Gods of Ragnarok, you've no doubt waited, hungry and frustrated, tempting people to serve you in return for rewards you never gave them.' He paused and turned his face full to them. 'How many others did you destroy before Kingpin was lured down here, I wonder?' He thought, then, of Kingpin as he had seen him, a poor shattered Deadbeat, poised at the brink of the well, still desiring to use the power of the medallion to reach down to the gods below and yet dreading to encounter once more their ruthless ability to take and destroy. 'Poor Kingpin,' he mused aloud. 'That's what you like, isn't it? Taking someone with a touch of individuality, of imagination, and wearing them down to nothingness in your service.'

'Enough!' The father god's voice boomed around the chamber. The Doctor had finally goaded them into speech.

'You have said enough!' the voices of mother and daughter god followed, eerily blending and overlapping with each other.

'Enough?' the Doctor exclaimed indignantly. 'I've hardly begun!' He drew himself up and spoke with all the strength and moral authority he had acquired over the aeons of his existence. 'You eat up vitality and imagination and give nothing in return. That is why I've fought the Gods of Ragnarok in some form or other all through time.'

'Enough!'

'You have said enough!' The gods were shouting now, blotting out his challenge and its reminder of all the battles that the Doctor and other free-wheeling and questioning spirits had fought against them across the millennia. The confrontation was moving fast now, the Doctor knew, perhaps too fast for comfort. But he had to keep their energies concentrated down here dealing with him in order that Ace and the others might be free to obtain the only weapon that could defeat them. He had never believed it was going to be easy, and it wasn't, particularly as events had forced him to play on their terms.

'You are in our dimension now, Doctor,' the father god called gloatingly. 'There is no appeal beyond its confines to any other.'

'Now let me guess what you want me to do.' The Doctor rubbed his chin in mock thought, judging rightly that mockery was after all the thing most likely to confuse and anger gods so given to demanding obedience and conformity. After a pause, he raised his hand. 'No, no, don't tell me. You want me to . . .'

'Entertain us!' the father boomed.

'Entertain us!' the mother followed.

'Or die!' The girl god's voice was the most chilling this time. Her two ominous words seemed to echo round the stone chamber and fade away only after a struggle.

'So long as you entertain us,' the father added, 'you may live.'

'When you no longer entertain us, you die.'

The Doctor eyed them contemptuously, remembering how many had suffered in trying to please them. 'Predictable as ever, Gods of Ragnarok.' He raised his hat philosophically.

And, out of nowhere, bright, brassy circus music filled the chilly chamber. He had no choice, he knew, so he might as well try to enjoy himself. 'After all,' he announced, as he prepared to give the performance of his life, 'whatever you've seen before, you ain't seen nothing yet!'

* * *

'Oh no, not that thing again!' Mags cried out in dismay as they reached the spot Ace had led them to. It was the site which Mags and the Captain had been excavating when Ace and Mags had first met. And there, apparently back to normal, was the robot head they had dug up with such disastrous results, giving the same deceptively sweet mechanical patter.

'Hallo, there . . . You look nice . . . Let me out please . . .'

But Kingpin had grasped what Ace intended and swiftly led the way towards the chattering robot. 'Bellboy built that head, didn't he?' he asked, drawing on memories restored to him after so long. Ace nodded. 'And Bellboy gave you that control device.'

'Dead right, Kingpin,' Ace agreed. The robot head continued to chatter ingratiatingly as they approached.

'I'll be ever so grateful if you let me out . . .'

This was hardly an object to be trusted, Ace had to admit to herself, but she did trust Bellboy and his gift. If the robot's destructiveness could be turned to their advantage, there was at least a chance of defeating their pursuers.

They did not have to wait long to find out. As they crouched behind the head, they heard the hearse draw up and the Chief Clown step out, followed by his assistants.

'Hallo, there . . . Like to help me out? . . .'

The Chief Clown's face split in an evil smile as he looked down at what he had been led to. 'Bellboy's greatest mistake!' he exclaimed in a tone of malicious wonder. 'What a place to choose.'

The trio peered round the head and saw that he was advancing towards them. Behind him came the robot clowns, impassive as ever, carrying Indian clubs in their hands. Or that was what they looked like; Ace had no doubt that some evil weapon lay concealed inside their wooden shells.

Now he was close enough, the Chief Clown was calling to them and they could see in his eyes a manic gleam. 'You may have the eye again, Deadbeat,' he cried, 'but you can't use it. You know that. You're not strong enough. You weren't before.'

'At least I tried,' Kingpin called back from behind the head. 'You just gave in to them.'

'Yes,' the Chief Clown exulted, 'And I'll get my reward. You won't.' He paused, waiting for their nerves to crack. 'Last chance, Deadbeat.'

The trio held their breath and waited. Ace held Bellboy's control ready, but she could feel her hand sweaty from the tension. The robot was prattling away. What if the device had been broken in her struggle with the conductor? Or if it no longer controlled the robot? And what if the robot no longer fired lasers from its eyes?

The Chief Clown was preparing to attack. Ace could see the gleam in his eye as he arranged the robots and it struck her forcibly, as it never had before, why the Clown was so scary, scary beyond even other clowns. He was crazy, crazy with desire for power, crazy with destruction, crazy with betrayal. He had believed in something once and he had let go of it bit by bit, letting go with it every part of himself that did not help him achieve what he wanted. That red smile and white face *were* the Chief Clown. There was no longer anything beneath.

'Deadbeat,' he shouted tauntingly, 'did we ever really believe in all that talk about peace and love?' As he spoke, he raised his hand to order his clowns to attack. The clubs were maces now, evil metal spikes protruding from them, spikes able to maim and to kill.

Ace pressed the control button. Nothing happened. The Chief Clown was lowering his hand. She pressed again. The clowns were starting to advance, and still nothing had happened. She tried once more, and to her intense relief, the robot leapt into action. Its powerful teeth started to snap. The eyes became animated. The hands started to reach out. And finally, to Ace's relief, the flame-like rays shot from its eyes.

'I'll get you . . . I'll get you, you'll see . . . I'll show you . . .'

The approaching clowns fell one by one as if mown down by a firing squad, their robotic bodies falling to the ground like ninepins. The Chief Clown, who came behind them, advanced a few steps more, the gash of a smile still unnervingly fixed on his face. But finally, he too was hit and collapsed to the ground. For a moment he raised an arm in protest and then fell back still.

'You just wait . . . you just . . .'

Could she stop it now she had started it? It took several heavy jabs at the control but finally the robot subsided into inanimate silence, teeth no longer chattering, eyes no longer animated, hopefully to stay silent and immobile for ever.

Mags breathed a sigh of relief. 'For a moment I thought you weren't going to be able to stop it.'

Ace grinned. 'Funny you should say that . . .'

Kingpin rose to his feet and led the way out of their hiding place past the crumpled clowns strewn across the ground. By the body of the Chief Clown he paused, and a look of intense regret entered his face. 'He could have been a great clown,' he sighed.

It was a fitting epitaph for his one-time colleague, but Ace could not help adding, 'I'm sorry. I've never liked clowns.'

Kingpin shrugged. There was no time for further consideration anyway. They had the hearse now, and that would speed them back to the Circus faster than they could ever have hoped to return on foot.

Kingpin went instinctively to the driving seat. Mags and Ace clambered in beside him. 'I only hope we get there in time,' Kingpin murmured as he switched on the engine and prepared to drive off. 'The Doctor's stronger than I ever was, but he won't be able to hold out against them on his own for ever.'

Ace nodded. 'He'll have a good stab at it though.'

12

Positively Last Performance

Tinkling music played incongruously in the vault-like stone chamber. It was music of such sweet banality that it was impossible to associate it with a struggle against time and for life, but that was what was going on in the ancient circus. Before the ever-vigilant eyes of the Gods of Ragnarok, the Doctor was pulling out all the stops to keep them entertained.

It was a delicate task as well as a dangerous one. In front of him the Doctor always saw an invisible clock ticking away the heavy seconds until Ace and their friends could return. If he tried too hard, producing the best he had at the start, the gods would become greedy, demanding more and still more, and he would not be able to give it to them. If he too clearly played for time, they would become restless and destroy him brutally with all the fearsome energy they had been storing here in their lair for so many centuries. He had to proceed slowly, without appearing to do so, performing skilfully and amusingly enough to keep them entertained, but not to make them either suspicious or over-demanding.

It was not a situation designed to show a performer at his best.

For the moment, to this tinkling music, the Doctor was performing conjuring tricks. He had produced bouquets from behind his ear. He had made coloured balls appear and disappear between his fingers in a dazzling variety of combinations. At one point nine balls had popped up in his hands simultaneously and he had thrown them up in the air and swallowed them one by one as they fell. Unluckily there were no doves or rabbits to hand or he might have been tempted to do something spectacular with them as well. Instead, he settled for a trick with a length of rope. A length of rope, he was explaining, had two ends. So too, he indicated with a smile, could his act.

A thunderbolt flashed angrily from the fingers of one of the Gods of Ragnarok. It warned him that he had gone too near the mark. They did not like being baited and their wearying demand for more would soon recommence.

The Doctor studied the rope that had been shrivelled in his hand. The invisible clock seemed almost to stop. He had to keep going, even though the Gods of Ragnarok intended that only his death would end this performance.

The Doctor dropped the singed fragment of rope lightly as if nothing had happened and looked up at the stone-faced figures, his face calm and unperturbed.

'You appear to find my act a little tame for your tastes, Gods of Ragnarok,' he said politely. 'But frankly, you're too greedy. You want everything at once. The best is still to come. In the meantime, rest assured, I do have something up my sleeves.'

And with a flourish, he pulled a string of brightly-coloured handkerchiefs, all knotted together, from out of his sleeve. And another string. And another. The reds and greens and yellows and blues of the handkerchiefs cascaded over the grim stone floor on which so many people had died.

And a black hearse pulled away from the excavation site and started towards the Psychic Circus.

Juggling. The Doctor had always enjoyed juggling. He had been practising his juggling in the TARDIS before the start of this adventure. Even somebody less enquiring than Ace might have wondered if he had been preparing himself for this very moment. But, unfortunately, Ace was not there to

131

ask him. The Gods of Ragnarok were there, though, willing him to fail.

The Doctor started with three coloured balls. And then four. Then five. And then, for good measure, an Indian club. Followed by his hat. The flying missiles made intricate patterns as they passed and repassed in his hands.

But the gods were impatient once more. An act like that held their attention for only a few moments while they took pleasure in its ingenuity and in the effort and concentration it cost the performer. Then they were again demanding something new. Something different.

The Doctor acted swiftly. With a deft gesture he threw all the objects up into the air at once. They all vanished in a flash, apart from his hat which landed neatly back on his head. The practice in the TARDIS had done him some good after all.

But this effect left a gap with nothing happening. It was only a split second, but enough for the Gods of Ragnarok. They sent thunderbolts shooting out from their fingers. The bolts broke into thunder and lightning above the Doctor's head. The sound was deafening and the air became dark and heavy with foreboding.

It started to rain. Feel the rain, the gods seemed to be saying. Feel it chill your bones. Doesn't it remind you of your mortality, Doctor? Of how little time you have?

The gesture might have been more effective if the Doctor had not found a simple riposte. He made a deft gesture and his umbrella, which had lain discarded on the stone floor since he had begun, leapt into his hand. His hand had barely made contact with it when it opened itself out to protect him. Not a drop of the water fell upon his head.

The black limousine hurried down the dusty tracks of the planet Segonax towards the Psychic Circus.

Escapology. Not, in the circumstances, the happiest of choices, but the Doctor did not have that many options remaining from his repertoire. And, after all, there was an element of real danger to escapology that would appeal to the gods' sadistic nature. The fire-eating had gone down a treat; so had the bed of nails. It was a pity that the gods lost interest in such spectacles so quickly and demanded more.

So escapology it had to be, and the Doctor was strapped into a strait-jacket with his arms pinioned, suspended upside down by a hook that hung from one of the chamber's mighty stone pillars, and struggling to free himself. It was dangerous, no doubt of that. One miscalculation and he would fall headlong to the ground, unable to break his fall as he crashed into the stone floor.

It was dangerous but it was not enough for the gods. Another thunderbolt cracked impatiently above the Doctor's struggling form.

'Doctor!' boomed the father's voice.

'Yes?'

'You are trifling with us.'

'Sorry,' the Doctor returned, still struggling in the confines of his strait-jacket, 'but I thought I was entertaining you.'

'You are very close to destruction, Doctor. We are tired of your playing for time. We want something bigger, something better.'

'Do you now?' With an effortless speed that surprised even himself, the Doctor freed himself from his jacket and fell to the ground, landing neatly on his feet exactly in the middle of the stone chamber.

He stared up at the family quizzically. The gods returned his gaze in a battle of wills. The Doctor did not need his invisible clock any more. The urgency in the air was almost tangible. And he knew he could not hold back any more. He would have to go into the finale of his act. And hope against hope that help would come before he finished it.

* * *

133

The hearse pulled up at the circus and Ace, Mags and Kingpin scrambled out of it and rushed into the vestibule. The wind practically blew them off their feet and the tattered posters and kites scurried around them.

They rushed into the circus ring. It was silent and empty. There was no sign of anyone or anything.

'The Doctor must be here somewhere,' Ace insisted anxiously.

Kingpin looked grave. 'He may already be in the Dark Circus below with the gods. There's only one way we can reach him.'

Kingpin had explained enough to Mags and Ace for them to understand what he meant. They must hurry to the stone chamber, and use the medallion there.

'But we must be careful,' Kingpin warned, fingering the medallion protectively. It was glowing slightly now. 'They're bound to sense its presence.' He stared gravely at the others. 'You do realize they'll do anything to stop us?'

'What can they do?' Ace demanded defiantly, but somehow she didn't sound completely convincing.

'Excuse me – do I have your full attention?' The Doctor enquired sarcastically. But his sarcasm masked a real concern. He had seen the daughter god sense something and lean across to her father and whisper to him. Power had flashed between their hands and had then disappeared into the void.

The Doctor had regained their attention now. But where had that destructive energy been sent? Could Ace and the others already be back in the circus? He had to hold the gods enthralled now or the energies would destroy not only him but his friends – and all hope of success.

'The climax of my act, Gods of Ragnarok,' he began, gathering all his energies, 'requires from you something you do not possess in large quantities.' He paused to allow his words to take full effect. 'I refer, of course, to imagination.'

134

He reached out with his hand towards the circus floor, and a small glittering piece of metal shot from the ground and into his hand. He held it up defiantly so the gods could see the metal was old and pitted.

'It all starts,' he began, 'with this tiny piece of metal.'

Ace, Mags and Kingpin rushed from the ring, across the vestibule and down the corridors towards the stone chamber. Perhaps it was a pity they did not have time to notice the corner of the wind-blown vestibule where Captain Cook's body lay covered on a stretcher, just as the robot clowns had left it. For, as they rushed from the vestibule, the cover started to move. The Doctor had not been wrong about the power the Gods of Ragnarok had sent forth. He had simply not been able to guess the form their planned destruction of his friends might take.

Led by Kingpin, meanwhile, they found their way swiftly to the stone chamber. They stood breathless near the edge of the dark well, gathering their strength for the final struggle.

Kingpin removed the medallion from his neck and advanced slowly, holding the obverse side up in readiness. 'Go for it, Kingpin,' Ace urged encouragingly. She and Mags had stood some way back, but it quickly started to become clear that he had overestimated his new-found strength and confidence. As he looked down into the abyss and raised the faintly glowing red eyeball to confront what lay below, he fell back trembling.

'I'm sorry,' he faltered. 'I can't. I'm still too afraid of them . . .'

'Kingpin, please!' Mags begged.

The two girls looked at each other in desperation. There was no other choice. One of them would have to try. They moved towards Kingpin to take the medallion from him. But before they could reach him, a figure stepped out of the shadows and knocked Kingpin brutally to the ground. He lay there, doubled up in agony.

'Perhaps I might relieve you of that.'

Mags gulped. The voice was all too familiar. Captain Cook emerged from the shadows, triumphantly holding the medallion. His face was a ghastly yellow, his eyes oddly blank but there could be no doubt that it was him.

'Captain!' Mags gasped. 'I thought you were dead.'

The Captain smiled a truly ghastly smile. 'I am, my dear,' he replied lightly, 'I am.' He stood there, the last and most grisly of the servants of the Gods of Ragnarok, holding the medallion in the palm of his hand. It began to glow with an eerie pulsating radiance.

The Doctor still held the gods transfixed by the story of the piece of metal. How it had once been part of a sword. How that sword had once belonged to a gladiator who fought and died in this ring to entertain them. Blow by blow, he spelled out to them the human suffering caused by their insatiable appetite for destruction. By the sheer force of his imagination he had transformed the battered scrap of metal into the gleaming sword the gladiator had once wielded before them.

The gods had watched and listened because nobody had ever dared to speak to them like this before. But what he had to say was unpalatable, and the Doctor knew they would demand his silence soon. He was totally dependent on his friends for his final response. He had calculated as best he could, but cast-iron certainty and inhuman calculations were for the Gods of Ragnarok, not for him.

The moment came soon enough. The gods called for an end to his impertinent lecture and demanded some fresh entertainment. Instead of responding, the Doctor folded his arms, the sword still held in his right hand.

'I have fed you enough, Gods of Ragnarok,' he announced calmly. 'You find what I have to say indigestible and so I have taken myself off the menu.' He eyed them defiantly. 'La commedia e finita. Curtains.'

The gods stared down in fury.

'We command you! You cannot stop!'

'Sorry. I just have.' The Doctor's brain was racing. He hoped that his desperate calculations might prove correct.

'If you do not continue, you will die.'

The Doctor shrugged. 'Maybe. Maybe not. It's all a question of timing, you see.' The Doctor had rarely said a truer word.

'Oi! Sarcophagus face!' Ace's defiant words stopped the Captain in his tracks. Desperate measures were needed now. Ace held the Captain's attention by her words for just a second. But it was enough. Mags appeared at his other side and with a deft kick knocked the glowing medallion from the Captain's hand.

It sailed up in the air for a second and then fell into the well and the darkness that waited there for it. The Captain collapsed with a cry of despair. The others stared down.

The medallion whirled in the vortex beneath them, then vanished from sight.

The sword flew from the Doctor's hand with a swiftness that took even the gods by surprise. He had hurled it up into the air, apparently as a last gesture of defiance. But, as it floated up in the air above him as if suspended in time, something materialized around it. When the sword fell back into the Doctor's hand, it was possible to see what that was.

The completed medallion, eyeball back in place, hung by its chain from the hilt of the sword. And the eye glowed with the potency which had been shut away so long.

The Gods of Ragnarok threw thunderbolts now. Thunderbolts that would have destroyed the Doctor under ordinary circumstances, reducing him to less than a pile of dust. But they had waited a moment too long and in that moment everything had changed. Now the Doctor held up the eye and the bolts were reflected at them! The more the Gods of Ragnarok threw, the more destruction they created to fall back upon themselves.

The walls of the chamber were starting to totter now. Dust poured through their crevices and the huge stone blocks began to crumble and fall forward. The gods gave out fearsome cries of agony and frustration, realizing that they could no longer reach the Doctor, could no longer feed on the energy of others. They had found someone strong enough and imaginative enough to turn their threats and their powers against them.

The Doctor continued to brandish the eye. The family themselves were tottering now. Their stone thrones were crumbling beneath them and they swayed this way and that before falling forward, blasted by the destruction that they themselves had unleashed.

They collapsed, finally, with hideous cries like those of a gigantic bull bellowing in its death throes. And still the Doctor held the medallion, while the vast pillars fell about his ears.

The whole of the stone chamber was shaking. Ace knew that they had won but knew also that they had to get out quickly. The trio started to run from the chamber but Captain Cook stood before them, blocking their path, his face livid with the exertion. They had no choice but to wait.

'You know,' he began in his familiar tone, gasping for breath, his face yellow and corpse-like, 'when I was on the planet Periboea, I met someone who walked around when he was already dead.' He moved forward towards the edge of the well. 'Personally, as an experience, I'd say it was very overrated.'

With a cry he disappeared over the edge of the well into the abyss. Boring to the last, Ace thought. But she kept her thoughts to herself. Mags watched horrified, until Ace led her gently away from the crumbling chamber.

The vestibule was like the centre of a whirlwind. Its walls flapped so violently that the canvas was becoming detached and floating off into the air. The kites and posters had already been scattered to the wind. All that remained fixed was Morgana's crystal ball. And then that changed colour, clouded over and exploded into a thousand fragments.

The stallholder talked endlessly of the day when the Psychic Circus disappeared. Everybody on Segonax did. How a huge wind had blown up and leaflets from the circus had been found scattered miles and miles away. How the big tent itself had sunk down into the ground and the ground had swallowed it up, never to be seen again. And how a strange man claiming to be a doctor of some sort had walked calmly away from the wreckage just before the Psychic Circus subsided into the ground for ever.

Coda

They stood on the brow of a hill watching the final end of the Greatest Show in the Galaxy: Kingpin and Mags and Ace, and, of course, the Doctor.

'You defeated them, Doctor,' Kingpin announced almost sadly. 'This is where it ends.'

The Doctor shook his head. 'No, Kingpin. This is where it begins.' He glanced to where Ace stood, staring down in fascination as the tent was sucked down and down into the earth. 'Enjoying the show, Ace?'

Ace looked him full in the face. 'It was your show all along, wasn't it?' she asked softly.

The Doctor smiled, but said nothing. How much he had known and when he had known it, he would never tell her. And, when she thought about it, it didn't really matter. The questions raised by her travels with the Doctor were far too interesting to have simple answers.

Mags was the most anxious person there. 'The Captain really is finished this time, isn't he?' she asked the Doctor pleadingly.

The Doctor nodded reassurance. 'But you're just about to start, Mags.'

'What do you mean?'

But the Doctor did not need to answer her. Kingpin had come up, his sadness transformed by excitement. 'I've been thinking, Doctor. Not just an end. A beginning . . .'

The Doctor nodded again in agreement and indicated Mags. 'And what better way for a circus to begin but with a wonderful new act?'

'Yeah! Weird and wonderful. Nice one, Professor!' Ace joined in enthusiastically as Mags held back unhappily. 'You'll knock the punters dead, Mags.'

'That's just what I'm afraid of,' Mags replied, turning pleadingly to the Doctor. 'What if I can't control it?'

'But you can, Mags,' said the Doctor, and they both remembered those terrifying minutes in the ring. 'You already have.'

Kingpin's reinvigorated mind was already racing ahead. 'And what about you, Doctor? You and Ace. Join the Psychic Circus. Travel the galaxy with us!'

It was a moment the Doctor had come to countless times before. The moment of farewell when others wanted him to stay. The moment of going gracefully. 'Thank you, Kingpin,' he answered gently, 'but we have other galaxies to travel.'

He turned to Ace with a look of complicity that she would always nearly, and yet never quite fully understand. 'I'm afraid,' he announced, turning back to the others, 'like Ace here, I have always found circuses a little sinister . . .'